THE RETURN OF THE OPERATOR

MARCOS ANTONIO HERNANDEZ

ISBN-13: 978-1-7320035-4-5 (Paperback edition)

ISBN-13: 978-1-7320035-3-8 (Ebook edition)

1

THE RETURN

THE OPERATOR LOOKS AWAY from his dog just in time to see a dead, rusted car right in front of him on the abandoned freeway. He veers his craft to the left but it isn't enough. A loud screech rings out as the right side of his craft scrapes against the car. The passenger side mirror is ripped off and tumbles to the asphalt.

Fenix barks when the scratch finishes leaving its impression along the length of the vehicle.

"If I wasn't busy with you I would have seen it!" the Operator says, in defense of himself.

Fenix turns on the passenger seat three times before he lies back down.

"Well you could have warned me if you hadn't been sitting there with your head on your paws."

The Operator reaches down to scratch Fenix behind the ears. His companion is a brown mutt the size of a house cat. His fur is a shade darker than white, but the dust keeps him a dirty brown. "You know I can't stay mad at you," the Operator whispers. He relies on the dog's superior hearing to catch the statement over the roar of their dilapidated hovercraft.

The graveyard of cars becomes denser as the two travelers

get closer to the city. Both hands grip the steering wheel as the Operator weaves through the skeletons.

"Agreed. They had all this shit and as soon as something better came along they didn't know what to do with it," the Operator says to Fenix.

The Operator wears a brown duster and a pair of goggles to keep the dust from his eyes, since his vehicle has no roof. The indentation around his eyes may or may not be permanent—he doesn't know for sure because he never has the goggles off long enough for the marks to go away.

A faster, more powerful hovercraft races by overhead. The Operator and Fenix both look up and watch the speedy vehicle as it travels towards the jungle of buildings that rise from the dust. It reaches the city and turns straight up between two towers.

"Must be an important one. I wonder what they were doing out here," the Operator wonders aloud.

The towers of the city had first come into view the day before yesterday. They stretch for miles in both directions and extend into the clouds above.

"It would be nice to have one of those, but at least we don't have to walk. We both know there's nothing worse than walking all day with a landmark in sight only to wake up in the morning to find it has been pulled away from you in your sleep," the Operator says to Fenix.

Fenix uses his hind leg to scratch behind his ear.

"I'll make a deal with you: get one and I'll drive it," the Operator says. He holds up his right hand to Fenix and bends his thumb.

Another abandoned car comes from nowhere and reminds the Operator to focus on the task at hand. The engine sputters at the rapid change in direction, but once its displeasure has been voiced, the craft continues to run.

The air around them becomes a dense haze when the travelers pass into the city on the ground level. Over one hundred levels of civilization above pump their polluted air down to the surface, where it sits below the third-level reclaimers. Years of this have left the air below the third level unable to be scrubbed clean. The cost of running the reclaimers to purify the air is the main reason so many people on the surface have trouble elevating themselves past the third level. The rumor is that the air above the eighty-eighth floor is a perfect blend of nitrogen and oxygen. Androids don't care, but it matters to the humans.

Sidewalks and roads have become one homogenous entity ever since the roads were made obsolete by vertical travel, and the residents of the city's lowest level take up the entire space between buildings on each side. The Operator provides a rare sighting of someone who travels by vehicle below the reclaimers.

Fenix jumps down from the passenger seat then jumps back up, agitated. He stands on his back legs and places his paws on the right side of the hovercraft to see over the edge as the two of them crawl through the crowd. It takes the Operator another dozen meters to hear what Fenix hears: the savage bark of two dogs up ahead. The sound emanates from inside a group of young people circled beneath a floodlight. At first the haze makes any estimation of the group's number difficult, but after continuing forward the Operator counts seven, all teenagers. The bones of a car are on the opposite side of the street from the group, and the Operator isn't positive there is enough room for his craft to pass between the group and the skeleton.

The Operator creeps his vehicle past the group and tries to see the pair of dogs in the middle of the group. The group pays him no attention until Fenix lets out an anxious bark. A teenage girl turns to see where the bark came from and meets the Operator's eyes. The whites of her eyes have been taken over by a vivid blue.

"What are you looking at?" the girl demands.

"Nothing, just passing through," he replies.

One final yelp and the dog fight is over. The rest of the group all turn their attention to the Operator and Fenix. The other six pairs of eyes all have the same blue sclerae. Now that they are aware of his presence and can move if necessary, the Operator urges his hovercraft forward with greater speed. He faces forward but Fenix keeps barking at his side.

"I know, but there's nothing we can do about it," the Operator says. He reaches over and pats his dog on the side.

The dog is inconsolable.

A loud noise comes from the right side of the hovercraft as it is struck. "What the hell?" the Operator says. He looks at the group of teenagers and sees the girl with a defiant look on her face. Her friends all bend down to find something to throw. Most of the junk they use as projectiles bounces off the side of the hovercraft, causing cosmetic damage, but one piece of metal thrown from behind gets into the cabin, bounces off the dashboard, and hits Fenix on the hindquarters. The dog yelps.

"I'm sure it hurt. Say the word and I'll teach them a lesson," the Operator says to Fenix. What lesson that might be he hasn't quite decided, but whatever the case the decision belongs to Fenix. The hovercraft continues forward but the Operator is ready to stop, get out, and do as he's told.

Fenix stays silent. The dog stares at the Operator to see what his human's reaction is, to see if there is any canine action he needs to take. Both human and dog wait for a sign from the other that never comes. The hovercraft carries its passengers out of range at the same time the teenagers decide the fun is over.

An old man sweeps the sidewalk in front of a metal door with a broom missing most of its bristles. His back is bent from the weight of time on his shoulders, and thin whiskers tickle his chest. He picks up his head and his blue eyes watch the Operator approach. Just before the hovercraft is even with his position on the street he drops the broom, shuffles forward, and stands in the vehicle's path.

The Operator slams on the brakes and glares at the old man.

"Are you okay?" he asks, loud enough for even old ears to hear.

"You dirtbags better be careful," the old man warns. A crooked finger points at the Operator and Fenix. "If you aren't I will be sweeping you from the street as well!" Blue eyes light up as he cackles, exposing a toothless mouth.

"And who will put us there? You?" the Operator asks.

"No, no, no. Not me, amigo. The ones up there." The finger points up well above the reclaimers and circles towards the buildings around them on all sides.

"I won't be here long, I'm just passing through."

The old man smacks his gums together. "Don't let them get you! It wouldn't be the first of Shad's warnings to be ignored by a stranger!"

The old man hobbles back to his broom, picks it up, and continues his sweeping as if the exchange had never occurred.

The Operator raises his eyebrows to Fenix on the passenger seat, and the dog lays his head on his front paws. They pass through two more blocks of crowded streets. The people all stare at the Operator as if they have never seen anyone use the road for travel. A young girl darts across his path, missing the front end of the hovercraft by the width of a breath.

The Operator turns the craft to the right to avoid hitting the child and applies the brakes just in time to avoid barreling into a cluster of people. A young man with his back turned is pulled out of the way well past the time when it would have mattered. Blue eyes all stare at the Operator.

"What's your problem?" the young man says with contempt. His hair is combed to the side and a blaster is visible on his belt. Something about him looks familiar, but the Operator can't put his finger on what it is.

"Sorry about that, a child ran in front of me. Are you all right?" the Operator says.

The young man stands tall, puffs out his chest, and begins to walk around the hovercraft like an inspector would if they were trying to decide where to begin their search for hidden compartments filled with contraband. The other members of his group follow his lead and surround the vehicle.

The Operator looks at Fenix. "Tell me when," he says. The dog doesn't move a muscle.

"It's my mistake. Don't worry though, I didn't hit her," the Operator says to the young man. He uses his chin to point to the young girl as she is inspected by her concerned mother, since both of his hands are kept on the steering wheel.

"And you think her life is worth more than mine?" the puffed-up young man barks. He places both hands on the front of the vehicle, right in front of the Operator. "You must be new around here."

"Just passing through," the Operator says. He looks down at Fenix. "Nothing? Are you sure?" he whispers.

"What are you looking at?" the young man demands to know.

"My dog, Fenix. We just came in from the badlands today and didn't expect the road to be so packed. Sorry about the scare." The Operator begins to move the hovercraft forward, slow enough so the young man can be sure to get out of the way.

"Me? Scared? Don't make me laugh," the young man says with a chuckle. The rest of his group joins in on the joke, each of their laughs fake and overemphasized. When the young man realizes the Operator has begun to inch forward he steps back and kicks the vehicle.

"Don't let me catch you around here again!" he yells out

before another kick lands on the craft. The rest of the group all begin to kick the exterior. The Operator and Fenix have no choice but to wait for the conclusion of their slow retreat. In time, the young man moves to the side and continues to land blows as the hovercraft passes.

The people not involved all keep their heads down and refuse to look at the group inflicting the damage.

The young girl who ran in front of the hovercraft stands still as her mother shakes her by the shoulders. The group follows the young man over to the mother and watches as he kicks the woman in the stomach. She doubles over and lies on the ground. The crowds continue to ignore the young man and his entourage as he walks away.

"Are you *sure* you don't want me to teach them a lesson?" the Operator says to Fenix. He can't shake the feeling he has crossed paths with the young man before.

Fenix lifts his head up, looks at the Operator, and begins to lick the spot on his rear where he was struck by metal.

"I can't stand when you don't say anything," the Operator grumbles.

The hovercraft lurches forward and a loud rattle comes from the engine.

"Great," the Operator says. He turns the craft onto the sidewalk. "Out of the way!" he says to the people who stare at him, unable to comprehend someone using the street for their vehicle. They move out of the way as the hovercraft continues forward in spurts. The machine exhales one final time and collapses on the ground in front of a large window with a loud scrape of metal on cement.

"Looks like someone around here wants me to teach them some manners. I hear you, amigo," he says as he pats the dashboard.

The Operator gets out of the vehicle to inspect where he has been deposited. The window glass is thick and clouded with mineral deposits. Unused pool tables can be seen inside.

"Let's go," the Operator says to Fenix as he opens the passenger door for his friend. The dog hops onto the sidewalk and together they go inside.

2

THE OWNER

"Was that you making all the noise outside?" an overweight man with a grey beard asks the Operator from behind the bar at the far end of the room.

The Operator wipes the dust from his jacket and Fenix shakes the dust from his fur.

"Must be, nobody bothers to play pool anymore. These two are the only ones who are ever in here," he says to himself with a nod to the two men at the bar, each with an empty glass in front of them.

"Haven't seen you around here before. Did you come from up there?" the bearded man says to the Operator. He lifts his chin and uses his lips to point to the levels above.

"I came from over, not up. We were just passing through," the Operator says with a nod to Fenix.

"From another district?"

"From the badlands."

The overweight man's eyes get wide.

The Operator walks around a table and runs his hand along the rail. "This your place?" he asks. He lifts his hand and blows dust from his fingers.

"It is. The name's Miguel. People call me Miguel. Well, nobody really calls me anything, because nobody comes. But if people were to come, they would call me Miguel."

"Wouldn't they? That's your name."

"Good thing too, because that's what people call me."

"Good thing," the Operator says. Fenix is at his human's heels as the Operator walks through the pool hall towards Miguel. All of the tables are scratched and cracked, the cue sticks are splintered, and there doesn't seem to be enough billiard balls to go around. The walls are covered with old sports posters, some framed and some not, all of them peeling and faded. Relics from the previous century.

The Operator stands in front of the bar and the two seated men don't move a muscle. He looks at Miguel with his brow furrowed. The question is understood by the bartender without the need for words.

"Androids. Came in one day over two months ago, sat down, and haven't moved since," Miguel says.

"Did you know they were androids?"

"When they came in? No. All I saw is their pointed teeth, so I knew they were from Sigma."

"Sigma?"

"One of the other districts. The city has three: Sigma, Gamma, and Theta. Above the reclaimers all that matters is which level someone is from. What matters down here is the district."

"They have pointed teeth?"

Miguel reaches over the bar and lifts the lips of the android closest to the Operator. "New fad. Young people in the districts distinguish themselves with body mods. Sigma has pointed teeth, Theta youngsters remove their nostrils. Blue eyes are the thing to get here in Gamma."

"I was wondering about those," the Operator says. He pulls

a barstool away from the counter and joins the two androids at the bar. He leans forward to look at the android's pointed teeth.

Fenix circles the spot on the ground next to the stool and lies down.

Miguel lets the android's lips go and wipes his hands on his pants. "What brings you into the city?" he asks.

"Told you, just passing through. We were minding our own business when a group of punks beat up my hovercraft. Fenix thought it was best I let it slide, but the hovercraft decided it had enough and broke down. If that's not a sign to stick around to teach these kids some manners I don't know what is." The Operator looks down and watches the dog wag his tail at the mention of his name.

Miguel shakes his head. "Things have gotten worse in the last few years," he says. He pours a cloudy green drink into a glass and places it on the counter in front of the Operator.

"I can't pay you for this," the Operator says.

"Serum's on me. Made by the Sisters right here in Gamma. Finest in the city."

"Serum?"

"None of the Stim the government sends down ever makes it to the people. Since everyone is worthless without it the Sisters found a way to use the reclaimers to collect the Stim exhaled by the population above. They call it Serum. Stuff's not as strong as Stim but it does the trick. Plus it isn't addictive like Stim. Once the Stim passes through the body whatever is addictive gets taken out. So with Serum we get a dose of the benefits without any of the side effects!"

The Operator swirls the contents in the glass. He regrets asking about the drink, but politeness forces him to accept. Before he left for the badlands he made a promise to himself to never use Stim again. Then again, he broke the addiction once, so he knows it's possible, even if it turns out Miguel is wrong about how addictive the drink is.

He gulps it down in one shot.

"Thanks," he says as he sets the glass down. The warmth provided by the drink trickles through his body. When the tingle reaches his hands he holds one up to inspect his wiggling fingers.

"You feel it?" Miguel asks with a smile.

"It's . . . different. You sure it's not addictive?" the Operator says.

"Positive."

"You say the Sisters made this stuff? What are they doing down here in Gamma? This stuff's good. They've got to be filthy rich."

"The Sisters and the government don't quite get along. Bacas, the chief Enforcer, stockpiles government rations of Stim instead of distributing them to the people in Gamma. He then sells it back to members of the upper levels. It's pure profit for him. In exchange for peace in the district he allows the Sisters to distribute Serum below the reclaimers, but he doesn't allow a drop to go above the third. It's so good he even serves it in his casino!"

The memory of how the Operator knows the young man from the street outside hits him like a shot to the head. Before he left for the badlands, when he lived on the upper levels, he had traveled to the tenth to buy extra Stim from him. At the time he was working like a dog and didn't have time to sleep, so he needed the boost to maintain his productivity. He was a much different person back then.

"I recognized one of the punks from earlier today. Bought Stim from him a few years back."

"What did he look like?"

"Rat-faced, hair combed to the side. The crew seemed to be his."

Miguel flexes his jaw. "Sounds like Greyson," he says through clenched teeth. He opens an antique cash drawer and pulls out a thimble. He slips it onto his index finger, presses it against his temple, and closes his eyes. "Look at the mirror and tell me if this is the guy you saw."

The scene on the mirror now begins at the bar, too close to be a reflection anymore. The pool hall as seen through the bartender's eyes. Front and center is the young man, both hands on the bar, barking orders. The seat where the Operator sits is empty.

The Operator turns around but nobody else has walked into the bar.

"Is this the guy?" Miguel asks.

"Yes, that's him. How'd you do that?"

Miguel pulls his finger away from his temple and the mirror returns to show the pool hall as it is. "It's my memory of the last time Greyson came in here." He takes the thimble off and puts it back into the drawer.

"Greyson," the Operator says, weighing the name on his tongue. "How long have the scanners been so small?"

"A few years now. The thing cost me a fortune."

"So this guy comes in to play pool?"

"No, I wish. The little shit steals bottles of Serum from me! He's an Enforcer, right under Bacas in the chain of command."

"Why does he want Serum?"

"I've never asked but I'd imagine he sells the stuff above the reclaimers."

"And Bacas won't do anything about it?"

"One, when the thefts first started I threatened to tell Bacas and Greyson said he would kill me if I told. Two, Bacas is the reason Greyson is the only one who ever comes in here in the first place. One day some teenagers tried to play pool without paying. I went straight to Greyson to ask him to do his job and enforce the law. Bacas himself showed up the next day to let me know that the teenagers were his men as well, even if they weren't part of the government, and that they could play for free because he said so. The teenagers stopped coming after that. I guess it was no longer fun for them since there were no rules to break. They were such good kids before they got involved with him! This place must have been blacklisted, because now nobody plays pool anymore. I sit here, day after day, alone with my thoughts."

"And with these two," the Operator says. He pats the back of the android closest to him.

"A couple of broken androids? Great," Miguel says with a melancholy chuckle.

"Sounds like Greyson needs to be taught some manners," the Operator says. He swirls his empty glass on the bar.

"Who's going to do it? You?"

"Maybe."

"Be careful. Bacas has a lot of people working for him, amigo. Some you may not even expect."

"Every punk in Gamma answers to Bacas?"

"The ones on this side of the midline do, in exchange for Stim."

"What about the ones on the other side of the midline?"

"Everyone over there works for the Sisters. Bacas leaves them alone as long as they stay on their side. If they do cross they are killed. It's a rite of passage for the foot soldiers who want to join Bacas's gang but aren't able to get into the government system for whatever reason. The government throws the murderers in jail, but once they get out they enjoy the same privileges as the Enforcers."

"The same privileges as Greyson," the Operator says.

"Exactly."

"Where can I find the Sisters?" the Operator asks Miguel.

"Why do you want to know?"

"Seems like all of us have a reason to remove Greyson from Gamma's equation. They might be willing to pay."

Miguel points behind him with his thumb. "They keep to themselves across the midline. They have a gang of their own too. They all wear white jackets so, naturally, they're called the White Jackets. I think it has something to do with the scientists who created the Serum."

The Operator takes a moment to think. "The hovercraft's out front and needs fixed. Know any mechanics around here?"

"Not for cheap," Miguel says. "They all work above the reclaimers. Nobody bothers with hovercrafts that stay this close to the surface. It will cost you just to get them to come down here and take a look. Seeing as you cannot afford Serum I would guess that your hovercraft is now another statue on the sidewalk," Miguel says. He holds up the bottle of cloudy green liquid and shakes it, his eyebrows raised.

The Operator slides his glass forward and Miguel refills it. He finishes his second glass of Serum and the effects are immediate. His muscles relax further and the room around him comes into greater focus. He catches a look of himself in the mirror and is surprised to see how relaxed his face has become. He takes the goggles off and rubs his eyes. No need to wear them without the dust of the badlands blowing in the wind.

"Guess I'll have to walk," the Operator says out loud, the statement directed at his reflection. He turns his attention to Miguel. "Think I could stay here for a few nights?"

"There's an extra room in the back. Right now it is full of boxes, but if you rearrange them there should be enough room for you to sleep there until you get enough money to fix your hovercraft."

"I'll take you up on that." The Operator gets up from his stool, leans over, pets Fenix behind the ears. "Stay here, I'll be back soon," he says to the dog.

"Where are you going?" Miguel asks.

"To see about making that money."

3

THE PLAN

THE OPERATOR LEAVES the pool hall and walks down the avenue back in the direction of the badlands. As he passes the floodlight where the dog fight happened he stops to inspect the bloodstains on the ground. Was the losing dog allowed to keep his life?

He turns left down a side street in the direction that Miguel indicated and crosses a street labeled ONE WAY. Through the haze a wall begins to materialize ahead of him. The wall extends all the way to the third-level reclaimers and is built out of old rusty cars. He backtracks, tries two other side streets parallel to the first, and runs into two more walls made from piles of junked cars. Back on the one-way street parallel to the avenue, the Operator heads towards the badlands. Every side street he passes has a wall in the distance blocking his path.

Lights glow one level up in the middle of the street ahead of him. As the Operator approaches he finds the lights are hung from strings tied between buildings. They mark the entrance to a bazaar set up at the intersection ahead. Rats are everywhere. They scurry between the legs of the patrons and a few of them are bold enough to brush over his feet as he walks. Nobody else gives the creatures a second thought.

He looks up at the billboards plastered on the buildings dozens of levels up. They advertise everything from sex androids to mouthwash. These products aren't available on the surface. Most people down here don't have enough credits to buy them and the ones who can afford them have ways to smuggle them down. The buildings reflect sunlight onto the surface by day and the neon glow from their billboards keep the city lit by night, so matter what time of day it is, the amount of light that shows up to fight through the haze stays the same.

So many people are in the intersection that if the Operator had tried to drive his hovercraft through he wouldn't have been able to find enough room to enter, let alone pass. Every person has the same bright blue eyes as the teenagers he encountered earlier. Pairs of eyes stare at him as he walks by, as if he is the one with an atypical characteristic. His head is held high as he passes carts that sell everything from repurposed clothes to food. More lights are strung beneath a large canopy that stretches across the entire intersection. Smaller pieces of cloth extend the canopy down each of the four streets that lead away from the center of the bazaar.

The Operator passes through the crowd and turns down the street in the direction of the Sisters' side of the district. The crowds are left behind, and a bridge rises up ahead. As he walks across, it soon becomes apparent the bridge is no longer connected in the middle. He stops at the chasm and looks down at the rails below.

"I think I could make it," he tells Fenix, even though the dog isn't with him. He eyes the opposite ledge. All of the rebar has been bent up and points at the Operator's head. Even as he paces left to right, trying to decide what to do, the metal poles are able to keep track of the position of his head. If he attempts the jump there is no question that he will be impaled.

At the fringe of the bazaar the Operator stops a dusty child. "Is there another way across?" he asks as he points to the broken bridge.

The child points down the one-way street that runs parallel to the avenue, towards the badlands. "The station," he says.

"How far?"

"Not far at all. But if you go in there the midliner will get you."

The Operator hasn't heard of a midliner before. "I think I'll be all right," he says.

The child holds his hand out.

"What?" the Operator says.

Small fingers squeeze the air. "For the information."

The Operator reaches into his coat and produces a plastic disk loaded with twenty-five credits. "Here," he says, and gives the child the white circle of plastic. The child disappears into the crowd.

The Operator chuckles to himself and shakes his head. "Everything for a cost," he mutters to himself. He leaves the lights of the bazaar behind on his way to the station.

"Where are you going?" a voice says behind the Operator. He continues to walk as if the question wasn't meant for him.

"I'm talking to you!" the voice yells.

The Operator turns around and sees the young man who was almost hit by his hovercraft. Greyson. "Just going for a walk," he says. With a long exhale he turns and continues on the path to the station. Once he gets the money to fix his hovercraft he can leave this city and this punk behind for good.

Greyson rushes forward and grabs the Operator by the arm. "Don't ignore me!" he roars.

The Operator turns around and looks at the hand on his

arm. With a calm refined by his time in the badlands, he stares at unnatural blue eyes. "Tell Bacas I went across the midline."

At the mention of his boss Greyson lets go of the Operator's arm. His mouth hangs open. "Bacas will kill you when he finds out."

"I'll worry about that. You just tell him," the Operator says. He leaves the young man frozen in place and continues his search for the station. After walking another block, alone, he finds a sign for the station pointing down a flight of stairs. The Operator turns back to see if the young man is where he left him, but the street is empty.

The Operator descends the steps to the station and ends up on a platform with dark tunnels that extend in both directions. The walls are covered with cracked turquoise tile, and piles of trash cover the ground. Rats come and go through a hole in the wall on the far end of the platform.

After a quick glance for the "midliner," whatever that is, he jumps down onto the rail and crosses to the platform on the other side. He climbs the stairs on this side of the station and makes his way onto an empty street identical to the one where he left the young man's threats.

The Operator turns away from the badlands and walks until he finds himself on the other side of the broken bridge. He looks at the bent-up rebar and realizes that the other side of the bridge is clear. He wonders if the bent-up rods keep people from the far side out or keep members of this side in.

He turns around and passes through a mirror image of the intersection that houses the bazaar on the other side. On this side of the bridge the intersection is empty. No lights, no rats, and not a soul in sight. He walks farther away from the bridge and comes to a strip of faded neon signs. Each of the signs were once a bright orange but now they glow with a small fraction of their former glory. The signs are utilitarian, and each states the function of the space below. There must be one restaurant, one brothel, one clothing store, and one tavern.

The Operator walks through the strip of establishments marked by metal doors. There are no windows to peer through. Windows on the second floor shed light on the street below. Pairs of eyes, made blurry by the persistent haze, watch as he walks by. Whenever he turns his head to look at one particular pair they disappear, giving him the impression that he might have imagined their presence.

The tavern is a good place to start. He takes a deep breath before he grabs the handle of the large metal door and gives it a pull. Locked. He puts his ear up to the metal and can hear the rustle of people inside like mice behind a wall. He balls his hand into a fist and gives the door three loud knocks. The noise behind the door dies out and he becomes aware of the suffocating silence on the street.

The door opens and a large man fills the doorframe. He hasn't shaved in a while and his beard is at the awkward stage every beard must pass through before it matures. "What do you want?" the man says in a gruff voice.

"Looking to play some cards. Is this the place?" the Operator says.

"Depends on what you are willing to gamble," comes the reply.

"Everything."

4

THE GAME

THE OPERATOR ENTERS into a smoky tavern. Blue eyes all stare at him as he walks through the room, led by the man who answered the door. The air is thicker inside than out and prevents the lights on the ceiling from illuminating the room to their full potential. The bar is on the right side of the room and the bartender wipes the same spot with circular motions as she studies the Operator. There is enough space in the room for five square tables, each able to seat four people, plus a large circular table in the back of the room surrounded by eight chairs. Each table is occupied by at least one person and everyone in the room has on a white jacket except for the bartender. Some wear white-rimmed glasses as well. It is hard for the Operator to make out faces, but it's clear almost everyone present is a woman. They all look much cleaner than the people on the other side of the station. The Operator becomes aware of his dusty appearance in comparison to everyone else.

The large man leads him to the back of the room. Together they stand next to the circular table and watch three people play poker. Two men and one elderly woman are too focused on the game to pay the spectators any attention. The hand finishes and the sole woman in the game pulls the chips she won towards her. All three players turn to inspect the Operator.

"Who are you?" one of the men, a giant even when seated, asks.

The man from the door answers for him. "He just showed up, said he's looking to play some cards."

"Is that so?" the giant says. A large stack of chips in front of him dwarfs the stacks in front of the other two players.

The other man at the table hasn't missed a meal or a snack in decades. Two chairs, one beneath each buttock, are used to support his massive weight. Thick gold chains rope around the rolls of his neck. More gold adorns thick fingers and adds weight to the constant tap of his digits on the table. Beady eyes look the Operator top to bottom. "Do you have any money?" he asks the Operator.

"No, but I am willing to put a year of service on the table. How many chips is that worth?"

"How do we know you aren't a worthless rat?" the giant says.

"You don't."

The three players realize the Operator is serious. They put their heads together over the middle of the table and confer in whispers about how much a year of the stranger's service is worth.

The Operator looks down at his side and remembers he left Fenix in the pool hall.

The three of them lean back in their chairs. "Two million in chips. No more. Take it or leave it," the man covered in gold says.

"I'll take it."

The elderly woman turns to the bar and gives the bartender a nod. Her soft face and grey hair reminds the Operator of what his mother might look like in her later years. Moments later a door behind the table opens and a man with the face of a weasel walks out with a briefcase in hand. "Give him two million in chips," the woman tells the weasel.

The chips are placed in front of an open seat at the table. The woman waves away the man who opened the door and brought the Operator to their table.

"Thanks," the Operator says to the group as he takes a seat.

The golden man introduces himself. "My name is Lorden and this is Prado," he says with a gesture of his hand in the direction of the giant.

The giant nods.

The elderly woman extends a hand and the Operator reaches across the table to shake it. "My name is Iris," she says. The skin of her hands is soft.

"Pleasure to meet you," the Operator says.

"Now let's play some cards," Lorden says.

Over the course of the next hour the Operator doubles his stack of chips, most of them coming from Prado. The giant still has the most chips at the table, but the Operator is able to close the gap with each passing hand. Another hour later, both Iris and Lorden have run out of chips and refuse to buy back in, but stay seated at the table. Lorden's heavy breathing and constant tapping on the table continues while Prado and the Operator finish the game.

"Will you sit still?" Prado says to Lorden, annoyed.

"Can't," Lorden says. "I stimmed before the game."

"What the hell did you do that for? It's just poker."

"Why not? I wanted to focus."

Prado shakes his head.

With wins in the next two hands the Operator puts a large dent into Prado's stack of chips and takes over the lead.

Iris deals the next hand. The gold of Lorden's rings flashes in the dim light as thick fingers tap the table. Prado looks at his cards and side-eyes the incessant drumming. He draws two cards; the Operator takes none.

Prado's entire stack collapses into the center of the table with a sudden, decisive push. The chips dwarf the amount already in play. "All in," he says. His blue eyes stare at the Operator to see if his opponent's face will betray his next move.

"Call," the Operator says.

The two men turn over their cards. The Operator has a pair of tens and Prado has nothing.

"You called with that!" Prado yells. His blue eyes flash red with anger.

"You were bluffing," the Operator says. Both his arms reach forward and sweep the pile of chips towards him.

"You have to let me win my money back. Make sure you are back here before the end of the week; we play at this time every day," Prado snarls.

"I don't *have* to do anything. I might come back, I might not. If I haven't left town by then I will gladly come to take more money off your hands," the Operator says, with measured coolness.

Prado stands up. At full height he is close to seven feet tall. "You better come back. For your sake." The giant storms off in the direction of the bar.

The weasel has crept up to the Operator's side unnoticed. "Would you like to keep your chips here for safekeeping or will you be cashing out today?" he asks.

"Cash me out," the Operator says. "I need the money."

The weasel disappears through the door behind the table.

Iris gives a nod to Lorden and the golden man hoists himself up from his two chairs to join Prado at the bar. "That was impressive," she says to the Operator.

"Thanks." The Operator folds his hands and sets them on

top of the table. If the stack of chips were still in front of him he would busy his fingers shuffling them.

Iris takes it upon herself to break the silence between them. "You said you might leave town?"

The Operator appreciates her attempt at small talk. "I'm just passing through and needed some money."

"Don't we all. Well, you have plenty of it now!" she says with a smile.

Something about the way the woman smiles with her eyes pulls at the Operator. He fights the need to tell her more about himself, unsure if he can trust her. If only he had brought the dog with him! Fenix is the one with the ability to sense these things.

"You can spend some of it at the bazaar and still have some left over. I haven't been there since Bacas banned us from crossing. It's been so long I forget what it looks like," Iris reminisces.

The Operator closes his eyes and lets out a forceful exhale as he shakes his head. He opens his eyes and words begin to trickle out. "Earlier today my hovercraft broke down on the other side of the midline and I didn't have enough money to get it fixed. I was coming over to see if I could earn the rest workin' for the Sisters."

"What kind of work did you have in mind?" Iris says with nonchalance.

The Operator hesitates, unsure if he should continue. He hears Fenix let out a playful bark.

Patient eyes wait for the Operator to continue.

"There is someone on the other side of the midline who needs to be taught some manners," the Operator says.

"Who?"

"Greyson."

"The Enforcer! I've heard about him. Bacas trusts him immensely."

"So I've heard."

"And what manners do you intend to teach him?" Iris asks.

"Whatever the Sisters had in mind."

The old woman leans back in her chair and presses her lips together. "Would you murder him?"

The temperature in the room falls as soon as the question leaves her lips.

The Operator regrets opening his mouth. "I don't know. If they asked me to . . . sure, why not?"

She steeples her fingers and holds them up to her mouth. "That might invite revenge from Bacas," she says to the ether. Her eyes focus on the Operator. "He's the real root of the problem."

"*I* don't have a problem with him," the Operator says. He remembers Miguel's warning and wonders if this harmless old woman could be working for the chief Enforcer.

Iris leans forward and rests her elbows on the table. "Then why do you have a problem with Greyson?"

No harm in telling her why. "He's the reason my hovercraft broke down in the first place."

"That's it? That's all it takes for you to agree to murder him?"

The Operator looks around the tavern. Nobody pays the two of them any attention. He turns towards Iris and his reservations dissolve with one look into her calm eyes.

"He sold me Stim when I lived on the upper levels. Clearly it was a long time ago," the Operator says, pulling at the lapels of his duster.

"And that's a problem?"

"You don't see how feeding an addiction is a problem? Nobody should be making money from the cogs in the machine."

"You know Bacas is really the one behind the smuggling of

Stim, don't you? Why don't you work towards eliminating the root of the problem?"

"How do you suggest I do that?"

"I would imagine it would start by getting close to him. Finding out his weaknesses then exploiting them," Iris says with fervor. She withdraws into her chair. "Just my opinion."

"And what about Greyson?"

The door behind the table opens and the weasel walks out to give the Operator his credits.

"What about him? If the head of the snake dies the body will follow."

5

THE ENFORCER

THE OPERATOR LEAVES the tavern with over nine million credits loaded onto five plastic disks, each identical in size. One red five-million piece and four blue one-million pieces. His mind is preoccupied with whether he should pay to fix his hovercraft or teach Greyson some manners. Before he realizes it, he has walked back through the deserted streets, back through the station, and back up the stairs onto Bacas's side of the rail.

Greyson and two young men sit with their backs against the wall of a building across the street from the staircase. All three stand up and approach the Operator when they see him climb up the topmost stair.

"What was that all about?" Greyson demands. The others stand with arms crossed behind their leader.

"What was what about? I was playing poker," the Operator replies.

"Nobody is allowed to cross the midline! And you just spent hours over there. Now you come back like nothing happened . . . Bacas will have your head."

The other two men nod in agreement.

The Operator hears Fenix bark at Greyson. The dog has

made the decision for him: the young man needs to be taught some manners. "Then take me to him," he says.

"What if we just kill you and throw your body into the tunnels for the midliners to eat?" one of the men behind Greyson, a blond man with a young face, says.

The Operator nods. "You could. But I have a gift for Bacas and I already sent a message ahead telling him to expect it. You wouldn't want Bacas to find out you were the reason he didn't get his gift, do you?"

Greyson raises an eyebrow. "What kind of gift?" he says.

The Operator pulls out one of the blue one-million credit pieces and gives it to the Enforcer. "This is for you. Take me to him and you can find out when I give it to Bacas."

The young man looks at the piece in his hand then back at the Operator. "How much is on here?" he says.

"It's full. One million credits," the Operator says. The three pairs of eyes ahead of him widen.

"Come with me," Greyson says, confused and curious.

The three men lead the Operator back to the bazaar, two ahead and one behind. Beneath the lights they turn and walk away from the broken bridge. Outside the cover of the last makeshift canopy the Operator can make out a bright glow in the distance, coming from the second level. Multiple bright lights materialize as their group gets closer, forming a word that can't be read through the haze. Bodies litter the sidewalk. Some sit against the buildings, some lie down, but all of their blue eyes share the same glazed look. Greyson and his men don't pay them any attention and walk by with heads held high.

Bright yellow bulbs outlined with red spell out "Suerte." The sidewalks in front of the establishment are empty. It's as if an invisible line has been drawn to keep bodies away. There are no windows and a solitary metal door sits below the bright lights. The young man walks right up to the door, throws it open, and walks inside as if he owns the place.

The brightness of the space inside burns the Operator's eyes. This is no smoky back room, no hidden hole-in-the-wall. This is an in-your-face casino, full of slot machines and women whose clothes leave little to the imagination. Cheerful music rings out through the space and a row of slot machines along the left wall make constant beeps and dings even though they aren't in use by a single person. Everyone in the room is focused at the bar, where two large-breasted female bartenders stay busy filling empty glasses. Rows of lights on the ceiling run the length of the room in a pattern designed to look like the light travels from front to back. Everyone is dressed in mismatched, tattered clothes. The Operator thinks back to the tavern across the midline filled with White Jackets and is struck by the difference between the two establishments.

Three round tables with green felt tops are aligned against the back wall. None of them are used for cards, and piles of empty glasses fill two of them. The third, in the corner farthest from the door, is bare save for one glass in front of the one person seated there. The hive swirls in front of him. He has a thin mustache, a sharp nose, and a sharp widow's peak to match. His eyes follow the young man's entourage as the Operator is led straight to him.

The group stops in front of his table and the sharp man looks at the Operator. His eyes stand out because they lack the blue color the Operator has come to expect.

"You are the dusty stranger who showed up earlier. I've heard about you," he says to the Operator.

"Good things, I hope. Are you Bacas?"

"That's me."

"I've heard about you too," the Operator says.

"And what have you heard?" Bacas says.

"Not much, just that you're Gamma's chief Enforcer below the third."

"I take care of the rats," Bacas says with disdain. The sharp man leans forward and rests his elbows on the table. "You've caused quite a stir in the short time you have been here."

"How do you know that?" the Operator asks.

"I know everything. I know you almost hit Greyson here, my best Enforcer," Bacas says, his eyebrows pointing to Greyson. "And I know that you just played a game of cards with the Elder Sister, Iris."

A Sister? The Operator takes a moment to remember all he can about the woman. He doesn't think he let too much information slip, but he can't be sure. "Word travels fast."

"Prado is another one of my Enforcers, though I've abandoned expecting too much from him. If you hadn't cleaned him out I doubt he would have told me you were at the poker game."

Greyson looks at the Operator with wide eyes before he turns to Bacas. "He said he has a gift for you."

The Operator reaches into his coat and tosses the remaining eight million credits onto the table.

"Did you win this in the game?" Bacas asks.

"I did. I gave him the rest for safekeeping," the Operator says as he points to Greyson with his thumb.

Greyson reaches into his pocket and tosses the million credits onto the table while attempting to burn holes through the Operator with his eyes.

Bacas laughs. "Prado said he will kill you for taking his money."

"Good luck to him," the Operator says. He waits in silence to see where Bacas will take the conversation.

Bacas handles the plastic disks before he sets them down in a neat stack on the table. "A fool and his money will soon part ways. I've told him many times to stick to business, but he insists wearing the white jacket helps them trust him even though everybody knows he is an Enforcer."

Bacas changes his mind about where to keep the plastic disks and puts them into his pocket. "It's better this money ends up with me than with the Sisters."

The Operator stays quiet.

"They said you had a dog. Where is he?" Bacas says. He leans over and looks on the ground to see if Fenix is next to the Operator.

"Left him in my room."

"You already have a room? You don't waste any time. I want to apologize for the way these idiots treated you earlier today," Bacas says, with a gesture towards Greyson.

"He almost hit me!" cries Greyson.

"Shut your mouth. I don't care about almost. This stranger seems to know where his loyalties lie," Bacas says to his second-in-command.

Bacas turns back to the Operator. "We always need help around here. How about you work for me?"

"As an Enforcer?" the Operator asks. Greyson storms off, and the two comrades linger for a moment before following.

"It won't be official with the government, but yes. I need an outsider's perspective. You be sure to tell me what you see and hear in the district and I will see that you are taken care of. Do we have an agreement?"

The Operator thinks and is about to respond when Bacas continues.

"Can you be here tomorrow?" Bacas asks. He extends his hand.

"I can do that," the Operator says. As the two men shake hands, the Operator hears Fenix growl.

6

THE SLEEPLESS

MIGUEL POURS the Operator a glass of Serum from behind the bar. Fenix is excited to see his human. The dog jumps up and places his front legs on the Operator's hip. The Operator responds with a hearty scratch behind the dog's ears. The pool hall is still empty otherwise, besides the two androids. There is no real way to tell night has fallen in the city other than knowing the time of day, because the glow of artificial lights keeps the streets below the reclaimers forever half awake.

"Where did you go today?" Miguel asks the Operator. He slides the glass forward on the bar.

The Operator ends the scratch with two quick pats on Fenix's head before he sits down at the bar.

"I met Bacas," the Operator says before he downs the Serum. "I work for him now."

Miguel picks up his jaw from where it fell on the floor. "How in the hell . . . Why?" the stunned man manages to say.

"How? I told Greyson to take me to him when I got back from across the midline. Why? Payback."

"You went across the midline and Bacas didn't care?"

"He cared, at first. But nine million credits changed his mind. That's when he offered me the job."

"You gave him nine million credits! That's more than enough to get your hovercraft fixed. Where did you get that kind of money?"

"Played a poker game with one of the Sisters." The Operator picks at something he feels between his teeth. He shows his teeth to Miguel.

"Clean. And you decided to give the money to Bacas?" Miguel says.

"In order to get on his radar. There's more money than that to be made on the feud between these two."

"Be careful, amigo. The Sisters might kill you if they find out you work for him."

"Noted." The Operator takes a sip of Serum. "Question for you: Are most of the White Jackets women?"

"From what I hear."

"The only men I saw in the tavern were the other two poker players, Prado and Lorden. Know anything about them?"

Miguel thinks for a second. "I've never heard of Lorden, but Prado is an Enforcer. Bacas requires an Enforcer on that side of the district and Prado is the first one who didn't get killed right away."

"Interesting. Got anything to eat around here? I'm starving."

"I do, in the back." As Miguel walks away he says, "You should've brought me some of those credits to pay for your room."

Plastic scrapes across the ground and the Operator looks down to see Fenix lick the bottom of an empty bowl. Water is on the ground from where it has spilled out. The Operator picks up the bowl, fills it with water, and sets it back down for the dog.

Miguel comes back with a bowl full of dark brown stew and

sets it on the bar. The Operator leans forward in his chair and begins to eat.

"I haven't forgotten about you, don't worry," the Operator says between mouthfuls of stew.

"Just don't get yourself killed," Miguel says.

"You're not going to eat?" the Operator asks.

"Already ate. Fed Fenix too."

"We appreciate it."

The Operator finishes his food while Miguel tells him about the days when business thrived. Miguel takes the bowl once it is empty.

"I'm headed to sleep," the Operator says. He walks away from the bar and leaves Miguel with the two inanimate androids. Fenix stays curled up at the bottom of the barstool.

"The boxes are still in the way. Rearrange what you need and don't break anything," Miguel says.

In the back room the Operator clears enough space for his body. He takes off his jacket, balls it up, and lies down on the floor with his new pillow below his head. After so long in the silence of the badlands, the ambient noise of the city keeps his nerves on edge. A full hour of tossing and turning passes before he decides to give up on sleep. He grabs his jacket and shakes it loose before going back into the main room.

Fenix lifts his head to look at the Operator, his eyes full of questions. Miguel wipes the glasses behind the bar. Even though no one visits his establishment anymore, the habits engrained in him from the times of prosperity have managed to stick around.

"Can't sleep?" Miguel asks.

"Not a wink," the Operator says.

"Do you need something to sleep on?"

"It's the noise. I'm used to the badlands."

Miguel looks up to the ceiling and listens. "I don't hear anything," he says.

The Operator puts his jacket on. "That's because you're used to it."

"Where are you going?" Miguel asks.

"For a walk," the Operator replies.

"There is nothing good outside at this time of night. Stay inside and let the dust from the day settle. No reason to let Bacas think you are sneaking around in the dark," Miguel says.

"Good to know," the Operator says as he walks towards the front door. Fenix realizes the Operator is about to leave and gets up to join him.

"Wait, I'm coming with you," Miguel calls out as the Operator opens the door.

"Didn't you just say there is nothing good outside at this time of night?"

"I'm tired of hanging out with these two all the time," he says, with a nod to the two androids. He grabs a jacket and puts it on before he walks past the Operator and out the front door. "You coming?"

"Want me to lock the door?" the Operator says to Miguel's back.

"Don't bother. Locked, unlocked, wide open . . . the outcome will always be the same."

7

THE RATS

THE OPERATOR and Miguel walk down the avenue, turn towards the broken bridge, and end up in front of Suerte. They stop to look at the people passed out on the sidewalk on each side of the neon lights. Even now, in the middle of the night, people can't be bothered to make it home. The Operator can't tell for sure if there are more people on the sidewalk now than earlier. The two men continue on to the bazaar in the intersection. None of the carts are open for business but people still occupy the space. It looks more like a meeting place, these people all here to rally for some unknown cause. Groups are clustered in pockets beneath the canopy. A rat scurries past the Operator and Fenix gives chase before a whistle brings him back.

"These rats are everywhere," the Operator remarks to Miguel as he watches a rat chase another right in front of him. Fenix watches these two go by but doesn't change course.

"Those are the wild ones. The well-behaved ones, the ones trained to send messages, are cleaner and larger since they are fed by the humans who use them. And they never run."

"They send messages?"

"Ever since the government began to monitor digital communications. People have used them for close to a decade now, if I had to guess."

The Operator can't help but think about how different life is for people on the surface. On the upper levels everyone uses messenger bots to send secure messages to each other. In a way, they function the same way as the rats. Each bot carries a message to the recipient and, once the message is read, the bot self-destructs. The upper-level version of communication, away from the curious eyes of the government, seems much more sanitary, but the bots can be just as much of a nuisance in their own way. He used to hear about accidents caused by bots at least once a week.

The Operator sees a shock of blond hair in the far corner of the bazaar and recognizes Greyson's ally. One of the men who has his back turned to the Operator looks like he could be Greyson. The Operator waits for the man to turn around to confirm that it is in fact Greyson before he points him out to Miguel.

"Greyson's here. He's still upset I almost hit him with my hovercraft," the Operator says.

"The other men with him all work for Bacas too, though not in any official government capacity. They're all addicted to Stim."

"Government Stim though, right? So they get paid indirectly by the government. Through Bacas."

Miguel takes a moment to think. "Yes, I guess you're right," he says.

A few of the people who walk around the bazaar wear white jackets that seem to be discolored on purpose. "The people who have on altered white jackets, did they once work for the Sisters?" the Operator asks.

"Some of them, according to rumors. See that lady over

there?" Miguel points to a middle-aged woman with red hair who leans against a food cart, alone.

The Operator nods.

"I know for a fact she has spent her whole life on this side of the midline. Somehow she must have come across a white jacket and decided to wear it. Maybe she made it or maybe the original owner was killed. Either way, she can't wear a blank white jacket. She had to put some color on it so Bacas's men wouldn't harass her. The White Jackets are notorious for how clean they keep themselves."

The two men are about to leave the bazaar when they see Greyson separate himself from the group. He begins to walk away in the direction of the station before he turns around and waves for his blond friend to join. The rest of the group stays where they are without explicit direction from Greyson.

The Operator and Miguel follow Greyson and the blond at a distance. They lose track of them at the edge of the bazaar, but Fenix continues towards the station. The two men look at each other and, with a shrug from each, make the decision to follow the dog.

The three of them catch sight of blond hair descending down the steps to the station. When they get closer, the Operator tells Fenix to take a seat ten feet before the stairs while he and Miguel sneak forward and look down. The blond is seated on the bottom step and Greyson paces in front of him, agitated.

From where they stand, the Operator and Miguel can't see the rails. "We should find someplace where we can watch the platform. Could we get into one of these buildings?" the Operator whispers.

"I don't see why not. As long as we stay below the third floor, none of the sensors will go off," Miguel says.

The two men go back to where Fenix still sits.

"We can't go up, the roof covers the rails. We won't be able to see anything. Is it possible to go down to the level of the platform?" the Operator says.

"Even when the trains still ran those were the worst places to live. Full of squatters and criminals."

"Let's see if we can find our way into a spot with a good view of the station."

Miguel rolls his eyes. "Lead the way, amigo."

They try to open a door into the building nearby and find it is locked.

"What now?" Miguel says.

The Operator looks to the building on the other side of the staircase. "Let's try over there," he says.

The two men peek around the side of the building to see if Greyson and his friend are still there. The bottom of the stairs is deserted. "We have to hurry," the Operator tells Miguel.

They rush across the gap between the buildings and can't find a door. They go halfway down the block before they find an entrance to the building. The Operator looks back and sees Fenix is still seated on the other side of the stairs.

He lets out a whistle, two low and one high, his own call to Fenix that the dog has heard countless times in the badlands. The dog races to his side.

Miguel grabs the door handle and gives it a tug. The door opens an inch but gets stuck in the doorframe. He gives it another hard yank and the door swings wide open, so loose on the hinges that Miguel almost falls back. He has to let go of the handle to catch his balance. The door hits the outside wall with a loud clang. Both men and the dog rush inside, and the Operator closes the door behind them. It takes two quick tugs to get the door to close all the way.

The group finds a staircase and descends one level down. Outside the stairwell they come face to face with a group of blue-eyed children. The children stare with mouths open, like the Operator and Miguel are the boogeymen their parents warned them about. They have the choice of fight, flight, or freeze, and each child has chosen to freeze.

"Where are your parents?" Miguel asks.

None of the children move or even bother to close their mouths.

The Operator grabs Miguel by the arm and pulls him in the direction of the staircase that leads to the station. "Let's go," he says.

The children turn their heads as the group runs down the hall, but all they see is Fenix. Saliva escapes their mouths as they watch the animal trot behind the two men.

8

THE MURDER

THE OPERATOR walks right up to the window at the end of the hall and peers through. "It faces the stairwell. We still can't see into the station from here," he says to Miguel without turning around.

"Let me take a look," Miguel says.

The Operator moves to the side and Miguel leans to the left in an attempt to see the station down the stairs to the right. "I can see a small sliver of the station from here but there isn't anyone there," Miguel says.

"Told you."

The Operator knocks on the door of the apartment between them and the station platform.

Silence. The Operator strikes the door again, harder this time.

"Who is it?" comes the harried voice of a man from behind the door. There is a scrape on the other side of the door and the Operator gets the feeling someone now watches him and Miguel through the peephole.

The Operator looks at Miguel, nods in the direction of the door, and backs up. Miguel should be the one to talk.

"My name is Miguel," the pool hall owner says to the door. If someone is in fact on the other side and watches them through the peephole, they have a full view of his wide face. "This is going to sound weird, but we need to look through your back window."

"What's in it for me?" the voice behind the door demands.

Miguel looks at the Operator. "Make something up," the Operator whispers. "I don't know what he could possibly want."

"How many others are out there with you?" the voice behind the door asks.

"I am with one other guy and his dog. We don't have much time. What will it take?"

"How many credits do you have?"

Miguel reaches into his pocket and inspects the plastic disks he pulls out. "Fifty," he says.

"Deal."

The door unlocks from inside. The door opens six inches and an old man looks at them from behind a chain lock. The Operator can't help but think how easy it would be to kick the door, rip the chain from its attachments, and force their way inside.

Miguel hands the plastic through the space and the old man snatches it out of his hand. He closes the door behind him and there is a loud shuffle from behind the door.

They stand there, helpless.

"Did he just take the money and block the door?" the Operator says out loud, more to Fenix than to Miguel. He prepares to kick the door down.

There is a slide of the chain and the door is pulled open as if it has to be dragged through molasses. Piles of papers slow the progress of the door as it opens. There is enough trash on the ground to reach their knees. Papers are piled high enough to tickle the ceiling outside the space required by the door to open. The smell of trash and human excrement reaches their nostrils. The old man is a hoarder. The Operator looks down and feels sorry for Fenix. His nose must be overwhelmed by the smell of the old man's misery.

The two men and the dog go straight to the back of the apartment. No window in sight. Piles of trash lean against every wall, reminding the Operator of the people against the building on each side of Suerte's front door.

The old man points to the corner of the back wall, where the guts of old machines are stacked high. "The window should be right there. You'll have to move some stuff out of the way," he says.

The two men hurry to move the trash. The Operator looks around for a bathroom door and doesn't find one. There isn't space in the piles for a bedroom door either. In the corner opposite the alleged window are clear plastic bags filled with shit. The stench seems more powerful now that the source of the smell is known. In less than three minutes the two men have cleared enough space at the top of the window for the two of them to stand on tiptoes and peer into the station.

Greyson is alone in the center of the platform. Two female White Jackets stand five feet from the platform on the rails below. "They work for the Sisters," Miguel says to the Operator. His voice is hushed even through Greyson wouldn't be able to hear them from in here.

"What are they doing on the rails?" the Operator says.

"Beats me. White Jackets who come onto the rails get killed. Or so I've heard," says Miguel.

The station's three occupants exchange words before one of the White Jackets bends over and picks up a box. She walks forward to the edge of the platform and holds the box in one hand while lifting the lid with the other to show its contents to Greyson.

Miguel and the Operator watch as a blond-haired shadow comes from the tunnel on the left and stands behind both White Jackets. He walks up to the White Jacket still five feet away and, in one quick swipe, slits the woman's throat.

A rustle inside the apartment causes the two men to turn around. The old man stands over Fenix with a piece of metal pipe. His eyes are alight with crazed desire and he picks his arm up to take a swing. Fenix barks. The Operator takes one quick step forward and pushes the old man into a pile of trash.

"What the hell is the matter with you?" the Operator says.

"You bring food into my house and expect me not to eat!" the old man yells.

Fenix continues to bark at the fallen old man. The smell of shit in the apartment doubles in strength, as if the old man's hunger has joined forces with the stench to overwhelm the nostrils of his guests.

The Operator takes the metal pipe from the old man's grasp, and Miguel looks back out the window.

"Take a look at this!" Miguel says.

The White Jacket who had brought the box to the platform is nowhere to be found. The Operator watches as the blond shadow grabs the box and hoists it onto the platform. The murderer climbs onto the platform, and together he and Greyson take a closer inspection of what the White Jacket had brought forward.

Miguel and the Operator stare in stunned silence as the White Jacket who had held the box comes into view. The platform hides her legs as she stands on the rails. There is a bloody hole in her chest. She aims her blaster at the two men and fires. Greyson stumbles back, his right hand clutching his left arm, and drops his blaster. It bounces on the platform twice before going over the edge onto the rails.

In a flash the blond man draws his weapon, and an instant later the White Jacket no longer has a head. Her body drops to join the other lifeless body on the dead rails.

The blond man runs over to Greyson and inspects his arm. Greyson stands tall, and blood drips from his hand onto the platform. He walks to the edge of the platform and looks down. The old hoarder throws a piece of metal at his two guests, misses both targets, and hits the window instead. Both men on the platform turn to look for the source of the sound.

The Operator and Miguel duck down behind the pile of trash. "Think they saw us?" the Operator asks the pool hall owner.

"If they did and they come to investigate we're fucked. We need to get out of here!" Miguel says.

The Operator tells Fenix to walk ahead and, together with Miguel, he rushes to the front door of the apartment.

"You aren't going to clean up your mess?" the old man says behind them with a sweetness in his voice that emanates from another part of his soul.

The Operator stops, turns around, and looks at the trash around him. "We did you a favor by uncovering your window. Consider the fifty credits a cleaning fee. You're lucky I let you live after you threatened my dog."

The old man lays his head back on the trash at his back and both hands hold his aching stomach. The Operator follows Fenix and Miguel out of the apartment and closes the door behind them. They rush down the hall, pass the blue-eyed children, and ascend the stairs.

"I think I can make this work in our favor," the Operator says to Miguel once the three of them are back on the street.

"Our favor? Who's we? You witness multiple murders and

want to get *more* involved?!" Miguel says. Sweat pours from his face, and it's obvious the man is shaken by what he just witnessed.

"Fine. I think I can make this work in *my* favor," the Operator says.

9

THE ALTERNATIVE

THE OPERATOR WAKES up early the next day. Sleep wasn't kind enough to join him for long; it was scared away after a brief visit by life in the city. Sleep remembers how there wasn't a sound but the wind in the badlands. The air was renewed by the breeze and the night sky hung overhead. Not only is the sky above now hidden from view, but the weight of the building above is palpable. The air is stale in the pool hall and the noise of the city never stops. It will take some time for sleep to get comfortable in this new location.

The Operator gets up from his spot on the ground between boxes. Fenix jumps around in a frenzy. He runs to the front door and back again, all in an effort to get the Operator to follow him.

"I'm coming, buddy, I'm coming," the Operator says to his canine friend.

He opens the front door and the dog dashes out. He runs to the building across the street and waters the concrete.

Faint rays of light trickle through the haze from above and mix with the artificial glow of neon lights. The sun has come up but there is no way to see its location in the sky. People are either still out or already on the streets, depending on if they stayed up all night or woke up early. Either way, without the force of the sun present in their lives, the people on the surface don't bother to follow a twenty-four-hour clock.

The hovercraft is still next to the front window but has been gutted overnight. Only the shell of the craft remains. "Well then," the Operator mutters under his breath.

Fenix runs back to the Operator's side.

"What should we do about this?" the Operator asks his dog.

The dog looks at the Operator and wags his tail.

"That's what I was thinking too," the Operator says.

Together they survey the road and watch people come and go. Every person ignores the Operator and stares at Fenix. Somehow these people walk by scores of rats without batting an eye, but a dog catches their attention. The Operator wonders if there are any dogs in the city besides the ones who fight.

The two friends turn and go back into the pool hall.

Miguel must have an extra sense about when his front door opens because, before the Operator can take off his jacket, he walks out from the back, shirtless but with a T-shirt in hand. His jeans and boots are already on.

"Where were you?" he says. He wipes both eyes with the backs of his hands.

"Had to take him outside to take a piss," the Operator says, with a gesture to Fenix.

Miguel looks at the Operator through puffy eyes. "Do you ever sleep?"

"Sometimes, but not last night. Couldn't convince sleep to make an appearance for very long," the Operator says.

"Well I'm going back to bed. Keep it down out here," Miguel says. He throws his shirt over his shoulder and goes back into his room.

The Operator looks down at Fenix. He makes sure the dog's

bowl has water before he grabs his duster and puts it on. "Stay here, boy, I'll be right back," he says to the dog.

The Operator walks back to Suerte. The crowds who occupied the sidewalk last night are gone as they sleep the day away. He wants Bacas to see him early in the morning in order to show his dedication. With any luck he will be there before Bacas and can wait for the chief Enforcer.

Suerte is quiet compared to how busy it was the night before. Bacas sits alone at his table. They aren't the only two people in the casino, but they are the only ones not asleep or focused on gambling. Nobody pays the Operator any attention. The Operator looks for Greyson as he passes beneath the casino's bright lights on his way to the back-corner table, wondering if the young man has told Bacas the real reason why his arm is injured.

Bacas has a stack of printed sheets in front of him and reviews them one at a time. There are fresh pencil shavings on the ground. "You're up early," he says to the Operator.

"You too," the Operator replies. He remains standing next to the table, across from Bacas. Men sleep with their heads on their forearms at the other two round tables. One man could be Greyson, based on his hair, but when the man rearranges himself the Operator sees that it isn't the Enforcer.

"Mind if I sit down?" the Operator says. How much does Bacas know about the incident at the rails last night?

Bacas rearranges the piece of paper in his hand and lays it down on the table. "Actually, I do. There are things I have to attend to."

"I'll be quiet while I wait. There is something I want to talk to you about," the Operator says.

"It will have to wait until later. I find that it's best to take care of these things early in the morning, while everyone else is still asleep," Bacas says, with a tap on the stack of papers in front of him. He looks at the Operator to make sure his gang's newest member gets the hint.

"Understood," the Operator says. He heads to the bar and takes a seat to wait for the chance to talk with the chief Enforcer. The bartender doesn't work this early and the Operator is sure that, as a member of Bacas's group, he could walk around the bar and help himself, but there isn't anything he wants. He looks around the room a few times, silent, studying the people who occupy the casino this early in the day. His glance lingers on Bacas. The man takes the time to flag any curious items on the page in front of him with a pencil before he puts the marked pages into a separate pile.

Bacas tears his gaze away from the piece of paper in his hand and meets the Operator's gaze. "You need to leave," he says to the Operator.

The statement from Bacas causes an idea the Operator didn't even know existed to bubble forth from deep within his mind. There is another way he can make the information work in his favor.

Without a word the Operator nods, gets out of his chair, and walks out.

10

THE ABDUCTION

THE OPERATOR SWEARS he sees a pair of eyes peer out at him from the pitch-black tunnel on his right as he crosses the midline. Maybe even two pairs of eyes, he can't be sure. The eyes disappear each time he turns his head to get a closer look. Have the owners of the eyes turned to run away, or are they still there, motionless in the darkness, while their eyelids cover the evidence of their existence?

On the Sisters' side of the rails, the Operator begins to keep an eye out for any White Jackets. If it wasn't for Miguel's warning he wouldn't have thought twice about another trip to this side of the rails, but now he can't shake the pool hall owner's words from his mind. What if he runs into Prado? Would Bacas allow one of his men to kill another?

The streets on this side of the district are deserted once again.

The Operator sticks close to the buildings as he makes his way to the tavern. The streetlights cast an eerie glow into the haze but fail to illuminate much else besides the air around them. Without the swirl of people, a gradient presents itself, the haze denser on the ground and thinning out with height. Haze flows into the metal grate of a third-floor reclaimer. If the reclaimers have been told to cycle through more air, could that mean production of Serum is under way?

Somewhere in his mind the Operator hears Fenix bark. He turns around. Two White Jackets are a block behind him. Neither of them bothers to walk any faster than the pace at which two lovers would take a stroll. The Operator continues on his path to the tavern. There is no desire to run but he also doesn't want to walk slow enough for the figures behind him to overtake him.

A block passes before he turns to check the location of the White Jackets behind him. No sign of them. He turns back around and comes face to face with two more White Jackets, different from the two who were behind him. One of them is Prado and the other is a young woman the Operator didn't see the first time he was on this side of the rails.

"Here to take me to the Sisters?" the Operator says.

Neither of them responds.

"Just a guess," he adds with a smile.

Prado slaps him across the face with the back of his hand. "You got some nerve coming back over here. You're a dead man, the Sisters know you work for Bacas," he says. His blue eyes flash with anger.

"Not yet. Why don't you take me to them so I can say hi?" the Operator says. He spits a red puddle onto the ground and wipes his lips with the back of his sleeve.

The young woman with Prado lunges forward and punches the Operator in the gut. An instant later Prado has put a hood over the Operator's head. This is not the first time the two of them have used this combination.

Instinct fights to pull the Operator's arms up and remove the hood. He calms his nerves and lets the two White Jackets tie his hands. One of the two leads him forward from behind with a hand on his shoulder. The strength in the hand is obvious, and if he hadn't just felt the woman slug him in the gut, he would assume the hand belonged to Prado. Now he can't be sure.

In the darkness the Operator wonders if the hood on his head matches their jackets.

They turn right, then left, then right again before he is led to a door. He can hear rusty hinges as a door creaks open.

"Watch your step," a female voice says from ahead of him. He shuffles his right toe forward to feel the threshold of the door before he walks over and through. If the woman is ahead of him, then the hand that leads him from behind belongs to Prado.

"Stairs," she says soon after. The Operator uses his foot to find the first stair and begins to climb. He counts. Ten, twenty . . . fifty-four stairs pass under his feet before his climb ends.

By the Operator's calculations they should be on the third level. The same level as the reclaimers.

The hand leads him down a hallway. Two right turns and the hand pulls him to a stop.

"Keep him here," the woman says from in front of him.

A boot kicks the Operator in the back of the knees and he falls to the ground, twisting so he lands on his shoulder instead of his face. With his hands tied behind his back it is difficult for him to get back up, but he manages to get into a kneeling position. He braces for another strike from Prado that never comes.

The Operator sits back on his heels to wait for whatever comes next. Time slows down. The smell of chemicals reaches his nose from beyond the hood and he can hear the faint gurgle of liquid rush by in pipes. Twice he hears claws scurry past and he assumes the sound is made by messenger rats. To confirm this suspicion, he listens for tails as they drag on the ground, but he never finds the sound.

Hands under each armpit pick him up and lead him forward three paces before they force him to make a quick right turn. The sound of boiling liquid, a thick sound made by the bubbles of a viscous syrup rather than the thin sound made by bubbles of water, bounces off the walls around him in the new space. Five steps into the room, he is forced to take a seat on a hard chair.

Someone, or two someones, leave the room and he is left with the bubbling liquid. The smell of chemicals is stronger and he wonders how noxious the fumes are. Is this some kind of slow death the Sisters have cooked up to use on their enemies?

The repetitive sound and the fumes in the room combine to make the Operator's eyes heavy. His chin hits his chest when he nods off. He isn't asleep for very long when the door to the room is thrown open and the footsteps of many people stomp into the room.

Someone's hands work behind his neck and the hood is removed from his head. Light blinds his eyes. He blinks over and over again until he can make out the face of Iris.

11

THE LIE

THE SISTER SITS in a chair right in front of him. Numerous metal pipes and heat exchangers feed into three brass distillation tanks against the wall behind her. Steam emanates from pressure valves located throughout the web of metal. A conveyor belt on the Operator's right side sounds out a constant whir as it carries open jugs of liquid to stacks of plastic bottles on pallets in the far corner of the room.

This is where the Sisters make the Serum.

The walls are exposed cinder blocks. A dark brown residue creeps downward from the ceiling. The only furniture in the room is four wooden chairs and a plastic folding table that needs to be cleaned. The Operator looks down through squinted eyes at the chair beneath him and wiggles against his bindings to inspect how sturdy it is. With a swift jump it would be possible to crack a chair leg, but he can't determine how it would improve his situation. His hands would still be tied, and the rest of the White Jackets would have no problem getting him tied to another chair.

He looks at the grey-haired Iris. Her vivid blue eyes are patient as she waits for him to adjust to the light in the room.

The chemicals in the air irritate his eyes and they continue to water.

"You wanted to see them! Here they are. Now start talking," Prado says from behind the Operator. His words are punctuated with a kick to the back of the Operator's chair, the force transmitted onto the Operator's lower back.

A new face walks into the Operator's view and stands behind Iris. The woman is young, slender, and has the eyes and nose of a hawk. She wears her black hair down, the longest strands reaching the middle of her torso. Her caramel complexion matches Iris's glow. A tattoo of bird feathers peeks above the collar of her white jacket. The Operator wonders what the bird looks like in full flight when it isn't covered up by her jacket and shirt.

"You played your hand well yesterday," Iris says with a kind smile.

"This is the one you were telling me about?" the woman with the bird tattoo says to Iris.

"It is," Iris replies. Her eyes never leave the Operator. "I'd like you to meet my sister, Klepsydra."

"Pleasure," the Operator says with a nod.

"You took a lot of our money with you. We heard you gave it to Bacas," Iris says.

"That's right," the Operator says. He licks his bottom lip and feels dried blood against the bottom of his tongue.

"Why would you do something like that?" Klepsydra barks.

The Operator presses his lips together and shakes his head.

"Well?" Klepsydra says.

"I'm not talking about Bacas with his dog in the room."

Iris looks past the Operator and raises her hand.

The Operator braces for a strike from Prado that never comes.

"You know that we don't allow Bacas's men to leave this side of the district alive, don't you?" Klepsydra asks.

"I've heard."

"And yet you still came across?"

"Here I am."

"Prado would kill you with his bare hands if we let him. You took a month's salary off his hands."

The Operator channels his inner Bacas. "A fool and his money soon part ways. Aren't you ever worried he will tell Bacas everything you do?" the Operator asks.

"Prado only tells Bacas what we want the man to know. Why did you come over here?" Iris asks.

The Operator tilts his head back to the man behind him. "Not with him in the room. You might trust him, but I don't," he says.

Iris looks behind the Operator and, with a sideways glance, asks the man to leave. Angry footsteps march out of the room.

"Better?" Iris says.

"Now start talking," says Klepsydra.

The Operator inspects both faces. "I have information the two of you might find interesting."

"It better be, or else we will let Prado come back in here and take care of you," Klepsydra says.

"I know who murdered the two White Jackets in the midline."

Iris turns around and looks at her younger sister.

Klepsydra holds her gaze steady on the Operator. "This isn't the first time our people have been murdered. When we tell the government, they direct us to Bacas. He'll pin the murders on one of the young men in his organization, they'll get thrown in jail, and when they are released they receive a lifetime of free Stim."

"What if I told you this time a government official got his

hands dirty, not just one of the foot soldiers? The government might find it interesting, to say the least."

"Bacas did it himself?" Iris asks.

"Not him. Greyson. You can relieve Bacas of one of his top men."

Feathers ruffle as Klepsydra flexes her jaw. "If you have proof Greyson got his hands dirty, the government would have to throw him in jail."

"And if we can prove Bacas tried to cover it up by pinning the murder on someone else, we might get a new chief Enforcer," says Iris.

The two women are silent while they think about the possibilities.

"Interested?" the Operator says.

Both women nod.

The Operator tells the Sisters about the scene he and Miguel witnessed from the window in the hoarder's apartment. The two women stare at the Operator with wide eyes while he talks. He can't tell if they are more surprised that Greyson killed one of them himself or that he was able to witness the entire ordeal.

"And where's the proof you were talking about?" Klepsydra says.

"I'm getting to that. Greyson and the blond shadow grabbed the box and left after Greyson shot the White Jacket. They never checked to make sure both of them were dead," the Operator says.

The Sisters have the hunger of revenge in their blue eyes.

The Operator begins the lie he has prepared. "The White Jacket who was shot in the chest dragged herself to the wall of the platform. She is your proof, your witness. She should still be there now."

"Why didn't you come to us sooner! We could have retrieved her hours ago. Who knows if she is even still alive!"

"I didn't know she was alive when I left; I saw her on my way over here to tell you about the murders. Unconscious, but I could feel her breath. I couldn't come sooner because I had to wait for some of Bacas's men who were around the entrance to the station to leave."

Iris studies the Operator before she says what's on her mind. "Why did you come to tell us at all? You said yourself you work for Bacas."

"I only work for him because of your suggestion. I thought you'd like to know, thought maybe it was worth something to you," the Operator says.

"You didn't get enough the last time you were here?" Klepsydra says. She shakes her head as she paces behind Iris.

"Give him half a million credits," Iris says to somebody behind the Operator before she turns her attention back to him. "We appreciate the information. If you feel the need to pass on any more information we are willing to listen. Make sure it is worth our time though; we can only guarantee your life one trip at a time."

Iris gets up from her chair. Klepsydra nods to the space behind the Operator and a hood is placed over his head.

"One more thing," the Operator says from the darkness under the hood.

The hood is removed so the Operator can say his last piece.

"Let me cross the midline well ahead of you. The men who patrol their side will find me and take me to Bacas. As long as you're quick there should be enough time for you to get in and grab your comrade without being discovered on the rails."

Klepsydra nods and the Operator is plunged back into darkness before being untied and taken from the room. He assumes the young woman who grabbed him from the street with Prado is leading him back to the station, but there's no real way for him to tell who controls their path. They move at a speed just past comfortable, through the building and back down the stairs. Tracking their route, he finds it is the reverse of the one they took on their way to the production room.

Memories about the last time he was above the third level replay in the Operator's mind despite his best attempts to clear them.

12

THE MEMORY

LIFE WAS different before the badlands. The path the Operator's life would take seemed obvious both to him and to those who knew him. Career, marriage, family: it was all laid out. There was no question about the woman he would spend his life with. They were young and too in love to see any reason why they wouldn't end up together.

He had grown up on the fifty-second level. The ability for vertical travel had driven the expansion of humans to new heights among the clouds, but when he was born the city was just beginning to settle into its new composition. Children were being born who never saw the surface of the earth. It seemed like the Operator would be one of those children.

Patrice was born on the fifty-second, like him, but her sights were always drawn higher. Their parents had set up their marriage when the two of them were children. Their wedding date hadn't been arranged, but ask anyone that knew them and they would agree, a better match couldn't have been made. They were each other's best friend. Attached at the hip. Comfortable both on adventures and in silence.

Something changed in Patrice when the two of them

returned from a vacation on the seventy-fourth level. Engineers had built this level so that anyone who visited would forget there was ever such a thing as separate buildings. One continuous floor of island paradise, the kind that only existed in history books. In order to get to the seventy-fourth, the young couple had to wait months for an access pass. Everyone who lived below the island had to wait for their pass, but if someone from above wanted to visit, all they had to do was grab a towel and ride the elevator down.

They had spent a week in love but as soon as they left it was apparent a small wedge was driven between them that grew as time passed. Patrice wanted permanent access to the island. She was no longer content with life on the fifty-second.

She urged the Operator to elevate their position. He agreed, of course, for her. After all, what he wanted most in the world was to make her happy. He dove into his work as a food inspector for the government. Long hours at side jobs for his superiors stretched on for weeks, then months. In order to work the long hours, he fed his addiction to Stim, even going so far as to meet Greyson on the tenth level to purchase more of the substance because the ration provided by the government wasn't enough.

The two of them, still too young to live together, had trouble finding enough time to see each other. She would tell him that once they made it above the seventy-fourth everything would change and they could finally be happy.

On her twentieth birthday the Operator took off work and went to her home to surprise her. He knew she was off work that day. A bouquet of flowers was in his hand, a new variant of orchids that had just been made by the horticulture splicers that worked near his office. Orchids were her favorite. These flowers were mixed with a form of plastic and would last for over a year without roots as long as they had water. Once the year passed, the smell of decomposition was designed to enhance their smell as the flowers decayed. His plan was to get her a new bouquet each year for the rest of her birthdays. In order to afford the prototype, he had to pick up yet another extra shift at work, but he convinced himself she was worth the cost.

He opened the door and walked in the same way he had done dozens, if not hundreds, of times before. His betrothed was seated on a chair, her chin touching her chest, while her father stood behind her. Her father had classical music on in the background and never heard the Operator enter their home. There was something wrong, something different, but he couldn't put his finger on it. As he walked forward he could feel his stomach begin to scratch and claw at his throat. Her father had a small tool in his hand and was playing with circuits in the back of her head.

Goosebumps raised from the base of the Operator's spine to the crown of his head. He wanted to scream, he wanted to run, but all he could do was watch. Whether he wanted to or not, he forced himself to suffer the sight of her father's work. After a long time rooted to the spot, his legs began to carry him out of the room. He closed the door behind him with a delicate touch, hopeful the father didn't hear the lock engage.

The Operator managed to make it back to his apartment and collapsed onto the sofa in his living room. His mother was home, and she could tell right away something was wrong.

"Is everything all right?" she asked.

The tears began to stream down his face before the Operator could close the valve. He broke down, the first and last time it had ever happened to him as an adult. "She's an android!" he yelled at his mother between sobs.

His mother took a seat next to him and rubbed his back. "What are you talking about?" she asked.

"Patrice! She's an android!" the Operator managed to choke out.

"Patrice? Are you sure?"

"I just watched her father work inside her head! How could you do this to me? Was I one of your sick experiments? Were you trying to see if I could detect an android right in front of my face?"

His mother worked as a programmer for the surveillance division of the city. She and Patrice's father, an engineer who specialized in android production, had both worked on the android recognition software when they became friends and set up their children's marriage. This was right around the time rumors began to surface that some androids had developed free will. The government promised ordinary citizens their jobs wouldn't be stolen, and the first step taken was to track every android in the city.

"I swear to you I didn't know," his mother said. Tears welled up in her eyes when she saw how the news affected her son.

The Operator shifted forward so her hand would no longer touch him. He didn't know who to trust.

"I swear. I am so, so sorry. I know how much she means to you." She closed her eyes, but tears still slid down her cheeks.

"Meant. She means nothing to me now," he said when he had regained control of himself. "And I meant nothing to her! She isn't even human."

He walked into his room, opened a bag, and began to throw clothes inside.

"Don't be like that. Maybe this is all just a misunderstanding," his mother said from where she stood in the doorway.

"I know what I saw. He used her to convince me to elevate! Maybe he hoped that if he had a daughter higher than the seventy-fourth he could leverage her position to raise himself too. What if I am happy on the fifty-second? She had me convinced that elevation was something I wanted. I have been working myself to the bone just to give her the life I thought she deserved and she isn't even alive!"

He tossed more clothes into his bag and looked around the room. "She deserves nothing from me," he said as he slung the bag onto his back and walked past his mother to the front door.

"Where are you going?" his mother said, worried.

"Down. I'm not playing this game anymore. Let him find someone else who can elevate her."

The Operator can still see his mother's concerned face disappear as the door shut behind him. He remembers fighting against tears while he walked down the stairs, lower and lower, until he got to the surface and the tears dried up for good.

13

THE CROSS

THE MEMORY of the last time he was above the third level still stings as he makes his way down once again, this time with a hood over his head and led by a White Jacket. He wonders if Patrice was ever able to trick someone into elevating her and gets mad at himself when he realizes he still believes she deserves it.

The Operator is pulled to a halt by the hand on his shoulder. The hood is ripped off his head and he is given a shove forward. Lost in thoughts of Patrice, he had stopped keeping track of his path and he now has no idea where he is. It's been a long time since he has let his addiction distract him.

As his eyes adjust to the lack of darkness, he can see stairs descend to the station ahead of him.

"Walk," a woman's voice says from behind him.

The Operator turns around and watches the White Jacket walk away, the same woman who abducted him from the street with Prado. He half expects to see the Sisters and more of the White Jackets in the distance, but he and the young woman are the only two people on the street.

The Operator walks across the midline, past the two dead bodies, and up the steps to Bacas's side of Gamma. He scans the street to see if any of Bacas's men are here to escort him to their leader and finds no one. In the distance he sees someone turn the corner, headed towards the bazaar and, maybe, to Suerte, but he can't tell if it is one of the gang members on their way to report his whereabouts to Bacas or just another citizen of the surface.

The Operator jogs to Suerte. He doesn't have a lot of time before his plan backfires and, if it does, he could find himself in hot water. The White Jackets are in a rush to grab the survivor they believe is on the rails and should get to the station very soon.

Bacas is still at his table in the back corner of the casino. A pair of twins grab the Operator, one on each arm, before he is able to get close enough to talk to the chief Enforcer.

"Tell them to let go of me!" the Operator yells to Bacas.

Bacas smiles as the Operator is brought in front of him. "I heard you were just on the other side of the rails. Didn't Greyson tell you what would happen if you cross?"

The Operator ignores the threat. "Listen to me: you need to act now. The White Jackets are on their way to the midline."

"They are? What for?" Bacas says. He leans forward and rests his elbows on the table, hands folded.

"There was a survivor from the exchange with Greyson last night. The woman is on the rails and the White Jackets are on their way to pick her up. If she talks she would be able to testify that Greyson was the one who shot her."

Bacas takes a moment to think. He knows what that could mean for his Enforcer.

Out of the corner of his eye the Operator sees Greyson walk straight up to him and punch him in the stomach for the second time today. He doubles over and tries to catch his breath. Greyson uses his good arm to grab him by the collar and bring him back up to full height.

"How do you know about the exchange last night?" Greyson demands to know. His blue eyes are tinted with suspicion and a dash of fear.

"The tunnels are full of curious midliners who will exchange information for food. I also know that the longer you stay here, the better the chance the Sisters get their White Jacket back."

Bacas pushes his chair back and stands up. "Supposing this is true, why were you on the Sisters' side? Were you the one who told them about the survivor?" he says through squinted eyes.

"You said you wanted information, so I went across to find out how much they knew. It was pointless though, they're all scared of you. None of them would talk to me," the Operator lies.

Bacas adopts a satisfied look. "As they should be. They are on their way to the station now, you say?" He looks at the twins who have a hold on the Operator's arms. "Let him go."

"You can't be serious!" Greyson yells.

Bacas walks around the table. This time it is Greyson's turn to be grabbed by the collar. Bacas himself holds the man, their faces inches apart, with no regard for the sling that holds the man's left arm in place.

"Does it look like I'm not serious?" Bacas says, with a calm to his voice that does more to terrify Greyson than any roar could achieve.

"No, sir," Greyson stammers.

"Don't forget your place," Bacas says. He lets go of Greyson and does his best to smooth the front of the man's shirt around the sling. His eyes count the four men in front of him. "I need six more!" he yells to the rest of the casino.

The gamblers in the room continue their games, but a dozen or so men make their way to the corner table. Bacas counts off the first six and dismisses the rest. The Operator doesn't recognize any of the men in their group beside Bacas and Greyson.

"Let's go," Bacas says. The group falls in line behind their leader.

Fenix barks somewhere in the back of the Operator's mind. He watches as the group of men follow Bacas to the front door and thinks that he should go check on his canine friend.

Bacas stops when he is halfway across the room and looks back at the Operator. "What do you think you're doing?" he says.

The Operator doesn't know what to say. The information has been passed along, his job is done. "Did you want me to do something else?" he asks.

"You're coming with us," Bacas says.

Greyson must be a terrible poker player because he doesn't bother or isn't able to disguise the look of disgust on his face when he sees the Operator fall in line behind the rest of the men.

Bacas doesn't move. He waves to the Operator at the back of the line. "Up here, with me," Bacas says.

Greyson moves closer to Bacas in order to block the Operator from standing right next to the chief Enforcer. Bacas stares at Greyson, annoyed.

"What the hell is the matter with you? Want to find out how I smell? Step back, you only have one good arm," he says to Greyson.

Greyson takes his arm out of the sling to test its integrity. The arm has a full range of motion but it is clear that each movement is painful. "I just stimmed, can't feel a thing," Greyson says through gritted teeth.

"Step. Back," Bacas says again.

Greyson moves out of the way.

Bacas points to the ground next to his feet as the Operator approaches. "Right here. I want them to see you next to me," he says with a murderous grin.

14

THE STANDOFF

"Stop sulking," Bacas says to Greyson while he leads the men to the station.

"I'm fine," Greyson says. His eyes stay directed forward and he marches on, stuck inside his head.

"If anyone should be grateful for the stranger it's you—because of him we get the chance to fix your mistake. Say thank you," Bacas says. He watches Greyson, waiting for a reaction.

The Operator takes note of the cruel streak in Bacas.

"Thanks," Greyson mumbles, his eyes still forward.

Bacas pats Greyson on the back. "Was that so hard? Now cheer up, we are on our way to fix this! No reason to be upset."

"I told you, I'm not upset!" yells Greyson.

"You sound upset to me!" Bacas says with a laugh. He nudges the Operator with his elbow, points at Greyson with his chin. The Operator doesn't crack a smile.

"All right, all right, I'll stop," Bacas says.

The groups stops a block before the steps that descend to the station. "Everyone have their Stim?" Bacas yells.

The group of men all reach into their pockets and each pulls out a syringe. They all nod. The Operator wasn't given any Stim, but it doesn't bother him because he hasn't used since before he left for the badlands.

"Inject!" Bacas says. The group of men all jam the syringe into their legs and depress the plunger to inject themselves with Stim.

"Let's make the Sisters regret their trip into the midline!"

Every man's eyes narrow and, if possible, the blue in their eyes becomes brighter. Bacas has his eyes towards the sky. The Operator follows his gaze and wonders which level of life Patrice calls home. He shakes his head in an attempt to clear the thought from his mind. A bad taste left over from a bad memory that has lingered far too long. He must remember to abstain from thinking of her so she can work her way back to the depths of his mind and stay away from his conscious thoughts.

The group jogs to the staircase and descends the stairs with noiseless steps. The Operator's body keeps him at the front of the group, but his mind is only half-present. The memory of Patrice becomes less potent as each second passes.

Bacas slows the group down at the bottom of the stairs so he can peer around the side of the building. He waves the entire group onto the platform at once.

The seven White Jackets on the rails are caught by surprise. They stand next to the two dead bodies and have just finished inspecting their fallen friends.

"What are you doing in the station? You know it's off-limits," Bacas yells. He draws himself up to full height and looks down on the White Jackets on the rails.

The Operator stands next to Bacas. He assumed both Sisters would be here, but he can only find Klepsydra, Iris must have stayed behind. When the Sister with the neck tattoo sees the Operator, she draws her thumb across her neck.

The rest of Bacas's men stand on the edge of the platform. All of them have their blasters drawn and aimed at the White Jackets on the rail.

The White Jackets who were crouched near the body stand up and stare at Bacas. Both groups are silent.

Bacas laughs when the group on the rails doesn't respond. "I know you know the rules. What will stop me from arresting all of you?"

"We haven't done anything, Bacas. Now that you're here we have a question for you: Why were our women murdered so close to your platform?"

"We had nothing to do with it. I heard there was a group of White Jackets on their way across the rails, so I came to see for myself and here you are! I can't believe it. If I wasn't here you could have made your way to our side and carried out whatever devious plans you had in mind," Bacas says.

"We had no intention of leaving the station, we just want to recover the bodies," Klepsydra says.

The Operator leans over to Bacas. "Look. The two White Jackets are already dead. They won't be able to get any information from them," he whispers from the side of his mouth.

Bacas leans back so that the Operator's head is between his mouth and the Sisters. "I see that. They must have moved the bodies."

"They had to, the one who was alive sat against the ledge. Either they moved her or the midliners did. Either way, she's no longer a problem."

Greyson enters into their whispered conversation. "Sir. We need to teach them a lesson. They can't just walk into the station without consequences."

Bacas looks at Greyson a long time before he nods. He turns back to the group of White Jackets on the rails. The Sister and her comrades still guard the dead bodies. There is no cover nearby and they are unable to back away from the situation. Klepsydra looks at the Operator with disappointment mixed with homicidal rage, like she had a feeling he would betray them and now he must pay.

Bacas stares at the group below. In an instant he lifts his blaster and shoots the White Jacket closest to him in the knee. She falls to the ground in silence. Her eyes are shut and her jaw is clenched so tight the Operator wonders how much force is required to crack teeth. However much it is, she has to be close.

The rest of the White Jackets stay silent and stare at Bacas. There is no way to count how many ways these people wish to kill the chief Enforcer.

A young White Jacket on the right side of the group creeps his hand towards the blaster at his side.

Greyson aims his weapon between the White Jacket's eyes with his good arm. "Don't try it. Bacas only shot her knee. I promise my shot won't miss your head." The other men on the platform nod in agreement. The young White Jacket drops his hand back to his side.

Bacas addresses Klepsydra. "Grab the bodies and back up slowly," he says.

The Sister puts her hand on the holster holding her blaster, and every blaster employed by Bacas aims at her head.

The White Jacket next to Klepsydra blocks her from drawing her weapon. She leans in to whisper to the Sister before Klepsydra decides against the shoot-out. She picks two of her group to drag the bodies back to their side of the midline. Two more White Jackets help their silent friend without a kneecap, one of them under each of her arms. They hobble together back to the platform on the far side of the midline.

Klepsydra is the last to make her way back. She looks

straight at the Operator and says, "We will not forget this," before she turns around and walks away.

Bacas laughs. "We're counting on it!" he says to their backs, as if the message was intended for him.

15

THE CELEBRATION

"A ROUND FOR EVERYONE!" Bacas yells when the gang is back in Suerte. The rest of the men whoop and holler in support. The atmosphere in the casino is electric and everyone is in a good mood after teaching the White Jackets a lesson.

The bartender pours shots of Serum while the twins hand out the glasses to the group of men. When everyone has their drink in hand they all raise their glasses. "Cheers!" Bacas yells, and the men respond with a "Cheers!" of their own before they take their shots of Serum in unison. The Operator places his empty glass on the bar and gestures for the bartender to fill his glass again. The rest of the men tell the bartender to keep the shots coming.

"Did you see the way they shook and trembled?" one of the twins says after his third round of Serum. His face is round and his rosy cheeks get more red with every drop of Serum he drinks. The men around him all laugh with him.

The Operator thinks about the quickness with which their memory has become skewed. From what he saw, the White Jackets stood motionless. Defiant.

Bacas cracks a smile as he watches his men celebrate.

"Ow, ow, my knee!" the other twin yelps. He hops around on one leg, holding his knee, while the other men laugh. He loses his balance and crashes into the table next to him. Empty glasses shatter on the ground. His face drops and he looks at Bacas, scared.

Their leader's smile disappears. He flexes his jaw before he erupts in laughter. The rest of the men join in on the joke.

After some time with the rest of the men, Bacas and Greyson go to sit at the table in the corner. The Operator has kept tabs on their drink consumption and knows that the drink in front of them is only their second glass, while the rest of the men are anywhere from four to seven deep. The Operator finishes his second and receives a third before he walks over to the table to join the two men. He pulls out a chair and takes a seat at the table.

"Who said you could sit here?" Greyson says.

"Shut up, Greyson," Bacas says.

"That was a good shot," the Operator says to Bacas. He raises his glass to his lips.

Bacas leans back in his chair. "You think so?" he says with amusement.

"You haven't seen anything, stranger," Greyson says. His voice drips with contempt.

"What the hell is the matter with you? You'll have to excuse him," Bacas says to the Operator. "I can only imagine his poor manners are due to the fact he is still upset about his sloppy transaction last night."

Greyson looks down at the glass in his hand and finishes what remains. He gets up and walks to the bar.

"I must say that the blaster he acquired in the deal last night works perfectly." Bacas pulls a blaster from his side and places it on the table, with the barrel of the weapon pointing at the Operator. The weapon is dark black with extensive modifications. A band of thick clear wire is coiled around the barrel.

The Operator leans back in his seat to take himself out of the direction of the weapon. "Was that the first time you shot it?" he asks in disbelief.

"It was. Worked like a charm," Bacas says. He taps the weapon twice.

"Brave. Everyone would have seen if you had missed—that was no easy shot."

Greyson sits back down at the table. "There is no way he would've missed. The new coil is magnetized and designed to equalize against any small movements."

Bacas smiles now that his secret has gotten out.

"Still, an impressive shot," the Operator says.

"I knew I wouldn't miss. I never miss," Bacas says.

"It's true, he's by far the best shot I have ever seen," Greyson says.

"Nobody likes a kiss-ass," says Bacas.

Another table falls to the ground behind the Operator and more glass shatters on the ground.

"Want me to take care of them?" Greyson asks.

"No, let them have their fun. It's good for morale," Bacas says. He takes a sip of Serum.

As evening turns to night, the men get more and more boisterous. Two fights break out and, each time, Bacas only has to tell them to stop once, without raising his voice, before the two men decide the fight isn't worth the trouble.

The Operator stays at the casino until the men are so drunk they have to be carried away. The Operator takes it upon himself to help one of the twins to bed.

"Where do you sleep?" he asks the drunk man.

The twin points to a door on the side of the room opposite the bar, in the middle of the row of slot machines. The Operator carries him through and finds a set of stairs that leads both up and down.

"Which way?" the Operator asks.

"Up," the round-faced twin says. He looks down the stairs in fear. "I hope I never have to sleep down there."

The Operator is directed to a room three doors down the hall on the level above the casino. After making sure the drunk man gets inside he shuts the door and walks back downstairs. Part of him wants to continue his descent and see whatever is below the casino, but he decides against it.

Bacas sits alone at his table. His men are passed out at the other tables and on the floor, wherever their good times left them. The Operator tries to decide which of them he will help to bed next.

"Leave them, they'll be fine where they are. You've done enough today. There's a room upstairs if you want it," Bacas says to the Operator. His voice sounds far away, as if he has something else on his mind.

The Operator has had a few drinks but not enough to prevent him from going back to the pool hall. "No thanks, I'll go back to my own room," he says.

"Suit yourself. Go home and get some rest. I'll see you tomorrow," Bacas says.

The chief Enforcer is left alone with his thoughts, his casino littered with the bodies of his men.

16

THE HOSTAGE

THE BODIES of more passed-out men litter the sidewalk outside Suerte. Fearless rats roam among the passed-out humans as if they have just as much right to the space as the humans who share their city. The thinner rats scurry about in their quest for food. The larger rats, the ones who look to be well-fed and cleaner than the others, have joined their cousins in the night, but their movements don't have the same urgency.

The Operator stops at a side alley on his way back to the pool hall to watch dozens of rats crowded around a pile of trash. The rodents climb over each other in their attempts to get closer to the source. As the stack of rats gets taller, the ones at the top come tumbling down in waves. The rats, taken as a whole, are a fluid that flows towards the trash and climbs up the side. The Operator walks up to the wave and shoves aside some of the rats with his foot. He expects them to scatter when they realize his presence but they ignore him as they try to get whatever food they can. City rats are different from the ones in the badlands. The ones in the badlands know they could be food themselves and keep their distance.

Right after the Operator passes beneath the floodlight

where he witnessed the dog fight, he feels a gun on his lower back. He stops in his tracks and waits to see what will happen.

"Walk," a female voice says behind him. She pushes the gun deeper into the tissues of his back with a force that tells him she isn't afraid to escalate the situation.

The Operator takes one step forward to balance himself before he again stands still. If he had to guess, this is one of the White Jackets, sent over by the Sisters. Did this person volunteer? It's a suicide mission if they are caught. Were they told to kill him, or are they here for information?

"I said to keep walking," she whispers into his ear through gritted teeth.

The Operator moves forward one slow step at a time.

"Faster," the woman behind him says.

He doesn't respond and continues with the same deliberate strides until he gets to the pool hall. He stops in front and the gun digs deeper into his back as the woman's momentum carries her forward.

"Why did you stop?" the woman asks. She doesn't bother to hide her anger.

"This is where I was going."

"What is this place?" the woman asks.

"A pool hall. I go here to unwind."

She looks through the cloudy glass and sees the empty pool tables.

"Let's go in, then," she says.

The Operator leads his captor into the pool hall and straight to the bar. In the mirror he can see that the woman has a mask over her face, but the feathers on her neck are easy to spot.

Klepsydra. It feels odd to see her without a white jacket on.

"Sit," she says.

The Operator pulls a stool out from under the bar. The legs

of the stool scrape across the ground and the Operator wonders if Miguel has heard.

Klepsydra casts furtive glances at the two androids with them at the bar. She points her blaster at the two of them. "Beat it," she says.

Neither of them moves.

She walks over to them and puts the blaster to their heads. Nothing. She waves her hand in front of their faces.

"Broken androids," the Operator says.

"You've seen them before?" she asks the Operator. She pulls the mask down from her face and lets it hang from her neck. She waits for a reaction from the Operator, a look of recognition, and seems disappointed when he doesn't give it to her.

The Sister pulls out a stool, two spots away from the Operator, and sits down. She keeps her blaster pointed at him. "You set us up," she says.

"What makes you say that?" the Operator says. He talks to her reflection in the mirror instead of turning to face her.

"Both our people had all of their spilt blood beneath them. They died where they had fallen, neither of them against the wall."

"I know. I had to tell Bacas in order to gain his trust," the Operator says.

"I knew you would tell Bacas! I told Iris many times, but she insisted we could trust you. I should have gone with my gut and shot you in the production room," she says, her voice trailing off at the memory of the missed opportunity.

The Operator looks at the blaster pointing at him. The same clear wires are wound around the barrel as the blaster Bacas used earlier. "How do those work?" he says, pointing to the coils. "Greyson said something about the coils being magnetized. Said it helps counteract small deviations."

Klepsydra looks at the barrel and seems to forget the real

reason she has crossed the midline now that the conversation has turned to her weapon. "The coils help but the real magic of the thing is the memory installed in the grip. The data is stored every time the coils are called upon to correct the trajectory. The more the gun is used, the better it can adjust future shots."

The Operator wonders why Greyson didn't mention this ability. Does the Enforcer even know about it, or did he just forget? "What if the weapon gets used by someone else? Their tendencies would skew the adjustment."

"Each blaster stores data from up to fifty unique individuals. It's a standard number; government-issued blasters store data from fifty people too. Those blasters only store the timestamp of the shots though, not information about any adjustments, since their weapons are strictly point and shoot. Iris could have designed the memory to hold more, but for once she agrees with the government and doesn't think more than fifty people would ever handle one weapon. She created the whole system herself even though she never carries a blaster."

"Is that the same type of blaster Greyson was going to buy the night of the murders?"

"Yes. Somehow he heard about the tech and offered an exorbitant amount of money for one."

"How much?"

"More than you can afford," Klepsydra says without thinking.

The Operator laughs and shakes his head.

Confusion covers the features of Klepsydra's face before being replaced with anger. "Wait a minute, we paid you for false information! Give the credits back," she says as she sticks out her hand.

"Can't give it back, I don't have it. Spent it at the casino."

"You're lying!"

"I wish I was."

Klepsydra slams the blaster on the bar in frustration. She realizes how much noise she has made and, even though she knows they are broken, looks at the androids and expects some sort of reaction. Neither of them moves.

Fenix barks from the back. The Operator tries to decipher which action the dog wants him to take.

"I know you still have them," she says. She looks at the Operator's dusty coat as if searching for the pocket he keeps the credits in.

"If you can find it in yourself to calm down and listen, we might be able to come to an understanding," the Operator says.

"What could you possibly have to say that would interest me? More lies?" Klepsydra says. She leans back in her chair.

"There was another witness the night of Greyson's double-crossing. A Midliner boy. If we can find him, we can access his memories and use those as evidence against Greyson."

"Lie! Why didn't you tell us about the boy before?" Her eyes betray the anger inside her.

"I told you, I had to gain Bacas's trust."

Klepsydra exhales and focuses on the man at the other end of her blaster.

"So your idea is to use a midliner? Nobody would trust them."

"We would have to extract the memory."

Klepsydra sits up and puts one elbow on the bar. "I would have better luck trying to get the government to extract the memory from Greyson, even though his Enforcer training taught him how to keep his memories encrypted." Klepsydra aims her blaster at the Operator's head. "Didn't you say you and your friend witnessed the murder? Why don't we extract your memories?"

"We didn't witness Greyson pull the trigger. We were distracted."

Klepsydra rolls her eyes. "It's always something with you."

"I'm telling you, the midliner's memory will work."

The Operator stays silent while Klepsydra comes to a decision.

"Assuming I let you live, you will find the midliner and bring him to us?"

"That's what I'm offering."

"And you will make sure he forfeits the memory to us?"

"Yes, I'll convince him."

Klepsydra eyes him with suspicion. She brings the muzzle of the blaster down to his chest and metronomes the weapon left and right. "How do I know you aren't going to double-cross me again? Why should I trust you?"

"For one, I will bring the midliner to you. There's no risk. Sit in the production room and wait, for all I care."

"How soon can you bring him to us?"

"Not sure. I can only search the tunnels between the times that Bacas has me working. I *will* find him though."

The Sister looks at him. The feathers on her neck stretch as she turns and looks at herself in the mirror. The metronome continues to tick. Klepsydra looks at her hostage and the blaster stops keeping time.

"You have one week. After that I will kill you myself," she says.

Fenix gallops down the hall and stops five feet away from where the two of them are seated. He barks at Klepsydra.

"Easy, buddy, I got this," the Operator says.

Klepsydra raises an eyebrow in disbelief. "I thought you only came here to unwind," she says.

"Something like that," the Operator says.

Miguel comes from the back. His eyes are swollen from sleep and he is midstretch when he sees the blaster aimed at his friend. His arms fall to his side. "Who the hell are you?" he asks the Sister.

She stands up and points the blaster at Miguel. She takes a step back and points the blaster at the Operator. With each step backwards she alternates between her two targets. She reaches the door to the street and aims at the Operator one final time.

"One week," she says before she disappears into the city.

17

THE DOG

"Who the hell was that?" Miguel says once the two men are alone in the pool hall. He grabs a bottle of Serum from the shelf behind the bar. "Want one?" he asks the Operator as he begins to pour himself a glass.

"No, thanks. That was Klepsydra," the Operator says.

Miguel stares at the Operator, his mouth open, and loses track of how much liquid is in his glass. He stops pouring when the surface tension of Serum is the only force keeping the liquid from spilling over the side. "You're lying! The Sister? I didn't see her tattoo."

The Operator reaches down and scratches Fenix behind the ears. "You weren't looking hard enough, it was there. Probably too focused on the blaster to notice."

"More like I was still half-asleep." Miguel leans over the counter and, pressing his lips against the rim of the glass, drinks the top portion of Serum, enough so he can pick up his glass without the liquid spilling out. "How did she find you?"

"Beats me. She stuck a gun in my back outside of Suerte. Made me walk ahead of her on the way here," the Operator says.

"The first guest you've brought back! What did she want with you?" Miguel says.

The Operator tells Miguel about his day, beginning with when Bacas dismissed him from the casino through everything that occurred with the White Jackets and the subsequent celebration.

"Sounds like she is more upset about being embarrassed by Bacas than anything," Miguel says when the Operator finishes relaying the day's events. He polishes off the rest of his Serum. "This is a dangerous game you're playing, amigo. If you aren't careful you're going to get yourself killed."

"I'll be careful," the Operator says with a nod.

"So you told Klepsydra that you will bring her the witness? I don't remember seeing anyone in the tunnels," Miguel says, his voice trailing off.

"Neither do I."

"So you lied? They will kill you for sure!"

"There had to be a midliner there who saw what happened."

"That's a big gamble. What are you going to do, march into the tunnels and ask each and every one of them?" Miguel says.

"I might. I'll have to go into the tunnels at some point, that's for sure. After that I'll have to rely on my good luck."

"You're crazy. The Sisters will have more reason to hate you besides just being a member of Bacas's organization when they find out you lied."

"Not the first time I've heard that. And yes, they might. I'll figure it all out tomorrow. Right now I need to get some sleep. A hard reset should help me figure out what to do next."

"I'm going back to bed too," Miguel says. He walks to the sink and rinses his glass. "Take the dog with you. I don't want him waking me up to go outside in the morning."

"Come on, Fenix," the Operator says. He gets down from

his stool and pushes it back under the bar. The dog raises his head and looks at his human but doesn't move. The Operator begins to walk to the back before he realizes the dog isn't with him. He snaps his fingers twice and the dog races to his side.

As Miguel passes by the two androids he pats the bar between them. "Goodnight, you two. Try not to drink too much while I sleep," he says.

The Operator falls asleep without taking off his clothes and wakes up to the smell of breakfast. He wipes the sleep from his eyes and walks into the main room.

"What time do you need to go to Suerte?" Miguel asks the Operator. He scoops beige porridge into a bowl.

"From what I gathered, the men report in the early afternoon," the Operator says.

Miguel slides the bowl across the bar and it comes to rest in front of his guest.

"Thanks," the Operator says.

"Sure thing."

The Operator takes a spoonful and blows on the food to cool it down. He takes a bite. "I figure as long as I am there by noon I will be all right."

"Are you going to take Fenix with you?" Miguel says. He puts a bowl of porridge on the bar for himself next to the Operator, walks around the bar, and sits down.

"Why, you don't want him around?"

"That's not it, I was just curious. You can leave him here again today if you want."

"I'll take him with me. I haven't seen any other dogs since the dog fight, but Bacas lets those rats run around all the time so I figure he won't have any problem with a dog."

The two men eat their meal in silence. After the Operator finishes his porridge, he places his spoon in the empty bowl and turns to Miguel. "What do you know about the midliners?" he says.

"No more than everyone else. Everyone up there," Miguel nods with his chin towards the ceiling, "assumes the surface is the lowest level of the city occupied by humans. They all forget about the people in the tunnels. Once everyone traveled vertically and the trains stopped running, the midliners took over the abandoned tunnels. Nobody knows how many there are."

"Interesting. Do any of them attack the people who cross the rails?" the Operator says.

"Not in this district. Not many people cross the rails in Gamma because of the feud between Bacas and the White Jackets. In other districts, where people are allowed to cross freely, there is word of an attack every so often."

The Operator nods, lost in thought.

"Worried they will attack you?" Miguel asks.

"Not necessarily. I just want to be prepared. I have one week to get the Sisters their witness."

"I heard." Miguel stands up and walks around the bar. He takes both of their dishes from the bar and puts them in the sink.

"When are you going to the tunnels?" Miguel asks. He turns on the water and pours soap on the dirty bowls and spoons.

"Today. Before I go to Suerte. I want to show my face in the station, just me and Fenix."

"Be careful. They aren't the same as us. There are different rules down there," Miguel warns.

The Operator and Fenix walk through the morning light to the station. Blood stains the rails from where the two White Jackets were murdered. Fenix walks to the hole in the wall on the far side of the platform to investigate the colony of rats that stream in and out. The Operator sits down on the ledge, his legs over the side, and stares at the blood, looking for patterns that don't exist. Fenix finishes his investigation and lies down next to the Operator, his jaw resting on his front paws. There is no movement other than a few pieces of trash that blow in circles from the cross-breeze created by the tunnels.

The humans on the surface look down on the midliners the same way the people on the upper levels look down on them. They cling to what little height they have over the midliners like a life preserver. There is no reason for the two friends to fear the tunnels. The Operator has already come from so high up that, to him, the surface and the tunnels are more or less the same. To him, the tunnels hold the same allure as the badlands. Part of him wishes he had gone into the tunnels to escape the demands of the upper levels instead of abandoning the city altogether, but he hadn't known about the tunnels then and he can't go back and change the past.

The Operator recalls the scene he witnessed with Greyson and the blond shadow. Throat slit, Greyson shot in the arm . . . didn't the Enforcer drop his blaster? The Operator leans forward, peers over the edge of the platform, and can't find the lost weapon. Did the White Jackets grab the blaster when they retrieved the bodies? Greyson could have come back later or sent someone to pick it up.

Fenix's nose quivers as he takes in the scents that blow in on the breeze from the tunnels. The Operator tries to remember how long they've been together. Has it already been three years? He remembers the first time they met like it was yesterday. He had set up camp underneath a rocky overhang when all of a sudden the dog showed up, a shadow at the edge of the light thrown out by the fire. Fenix was skittish at first, but the promise of food took the edge off. It took a long time for the dog to get comfortable enough to let the Operator touch him, but, over time, the dog warmed to him. After only a few months together they had achieved the level of trust in each other they have now. The rest of their years together were spent learning to interpret each other's subtle signals and desires.

The Operator wonders what the dog smells from the tunnels. Is it food? Are there humans? He waits for the dog to give him a sign about what to do next.

The dog's nose continues to quiver.

He looks to the tunnel on his right and thinks he sees the flash of a pair of eyes before they disappear into the darkness. The eyes must know he is in the station. Do they know he works for Bacas? If the Operator had to guess he would say they don't care about surface rivalries. They only care about why this man spends so much time around the entrance to their tunnels.

Fenix picks up his head and stares into the darkness of the tunnel on their right. He takes a long sniff, stands up, and walks down the platform towards the source. Someone is close.

The Operator stands up and whistles for Fenix to come back to his side. He has the information he came for. "Let's go," he says.

If there is a midliner who has made it their business to watch a man and his dog sit on the platform, there is a good chance there is a midliner who saw the exchange between Greyson and the White Jackets. The hard part will be to convince them to give up the memory.

18

THE ELEVATION

SUERTE IS a hive of activity when the Operator arrives. Since it isn't even lunchtime yet he expected the casino to still be quiet, but the gang members present all buzz around, each involved in some important task. The only ones who sit still are the gamblers. They can't be bothered to pay attention to anything other than their games. The Operator gets jostled twice on his way to the back of the room. Greyson sits at the back-corner table with his back to the rest of the room, a computer on the table in front of him. His left arm is back in a sling but there is enough slack for his hand to reach the keyboard.

"What's going on?" the Operator says.

Greyson turns around, takes one look at the Operator, and turns back to the computer. The Operator stands over the young man and watches his fingers fly over the keyboard. The silence lasts for a few moments and the Operator wonders when Greyson will tell him to leave.

"A government carrier full of Stim has been hijacked," Greyson says.

"A carrier? Where was it sent from?" the Operator asks.

"The fiftieth. That's where our Stim shipments come from," Greyson says, annoyed at having to explain simple facts.

The Operator watches as Greyson sends out message after message. No reason to use rats to hide these messages since the government must know, or will soon find out, about the hijacked shipment.

"Were you able to recover the Stim?"

"No."

"How'd it happen?"

Greyson measures the Operator with a look to decide how much information to share. "Right after the carrier dropped below the twentieth it was swarmed by hijackers who descended on ropes from above. They alternated jumping on each wing until the stabilizer systems went haywire. The ship ran into a building and fell to the surface."

"Were any of them caught?"

"No, the jumpers ran along the buildings at the end of their ropes and made it back inside. We are looking through the surveillance footage now, but those guys aren't our problem. Our job is to figure out who swooped in on the ground and took all the cargo from the crash site. Start to finish, the operation took less than three minutes."

"Then let's go get the Stim back," the Operator says to Greyson. He looks around at the gang in the casino and can feel the restless energy in the room. "Why is everyone still here? It shouldn't be hard to find whoever did this."

"It's not that simple. The attack wasn't on our side of Gamma. It happened on *their* side. If we can find evidence of involvement by the White Jackets we can take action against them, but there is no record of any of them above the third level."

"So?" the Operator says.

"It means they had help from above. The government wants us to find out who it was before we do anything."

"I get the feeling that nothing happens on their side of the midline without their knowledge," the Operator says.

"I agree, but as much as I want to teach them a lesson, we have to let the order come from higher up," Greyson says, annoyed at his impotence.

"So there really isn't anything we can do."

"I tried to access the cameras but they were all blocked at the time of recovery. The most we can do right now is take action against whoever blocked the cameras, but there isn't any evidence the White Jackets had a part in that either. For now, we wait. Unless Bacas has another idea."

Greyson must see movement through the corner of his eye because he looks down at Fenix. "You brought the dog with you today," he says.

"I did."

"There aren't many dogs around these days. Keep an eye on him. Bacas has been known to use small dogs for target practice."

The Operator can't tell if this is Greyson's idea of a joke.

A door in the middle of the slot machines opens and everyone turns to see Bacas enter the casino. The whole room waits to see the type of mood their leader is in. The Operator hopes he isn't in the mood for target practice.

"Back to work," Bacas says to his men. The men follow their leader's order and scurry away.

Bacas walks to his chair in the back corner of the room. Greyson stops his work on the computer as his boss takes a seat. The Operator pulls out a chair and sits down as well.

Greyson glares at the Operator before he turns to Bacas. "What are we going to do?" he asks.

"We? I know what I am going to do. I am going to eat some food. Might have some dessert after."

Greyson looks agitated and Bacas couldn't care less. "What are we going to do about the Stim heist?" Greyson clarifies.

"We have enough Stim in reserve, don't we?" Bacas says. The Operator is sure the Enforcer already knows the answer.

"Yes, we have enough to miss . . ." Greyson performs some mental calculations, ". . . ten deliveries. But don't you think we should teach the Sisters a lesson?"

"Last night wasn't enough for you? If we push them too far they are bound to retaliate," Bacas says.

A plate of meat and rice is set down in front of Bacas and he begins to eat.

"Seems desperate to me," the Operator says. He leans back in his chair.

"What do you know? It isn't desperate to impose order in the district," snaps Greyson.

Bacas swallows the food in his mouth, looks at the Operator, then looks at Greyson. "Stop talking and listen for once," he tells the young man. He turns back to the Operator. "What do you mean?"

"I didn't mean any action we take would be desperate. I meant that their actions are desperate. Reeks of desperation, actually. To attack a government carrier is a risky move. Whoever did it is now exposed to government consequences. And the way they did it? If they had money they would have hacked the carrier, unloaded it, and left the ship intact. Instead, they did it with brute force. They have manpower, and lots of it."

"What are you getting at?" Bacas says through a mouthful of food.

"Whoever did this needed those Stim packs."

Greyson begins to clap. At first he leaves space between

each clap, but over time his hands pick up speed. The rest of the gang all watch the three men seated around the back-corner table. Bacas stabs the meat on his plate with his fork.

"This is a great theory. A beautiful theory," Greyson says with a grin when he is done clapping. "But it doesn't change the fact that we need to take action against whoever did this!"

Bacas leaves his fork, laden with food, an inch from his face. He sets the fork down on the plate instead of taking a bite and folds his hands together. "How many times do I have to tell you? Stop. Talking." In one swift movement he stands up and pulls a blaster from the holster at his side. He points it at Greyson's head. The grin on the young man's face disappears.

"First, you screw up the exchange in the station and almost launch an official investigation into your actions. Now, here you are, talking about taking action when the government told us not to. You are completely unaware of how foolish your mouth makes you seem! I'm only going to tell you this one final time, so pay attention: Stop. Talking."

Bacas holsters his weapon, sits back down, and puts the forkful of food into his mouth.

"What do you think we should do?" Bacas asks the Operator.

The bustle in the casino returns as the rest of the gang returns to their business. Greyson tries to kill the Operator with his stare. If Bacas wasn't present there is a good chance he would lunge at the Operator, even with his arm in a sling.

"Honestly, I think we do nothing. That much Stim will benefit a lot of people, a lot of people who might have a problem with any action we take. Their desperation will show itself again."

Greyson couldn't look more unhappy if he tried. Bacas looks at him and raises his eyebrows, baiting the man to talk.

Greyson's face gets red from the effort it takes to hold his opinion inside.

"I agree," Bacas says. He puts his napkin over the food left on his plate. "The government will take care of extra security on the next carrier. Unless they tell us to take specific action, we will wait for the thieves to show themselves again. When they stick their necks out we will be ready to chop off their heads."

Greyson stands up from the table. The rest of the gang watches him storm out the front door. Greyson's blond friend looks at Bacas for direction. Bacas nods towards the door and the blond man follows Greyson.

19

THE SLIP

"Have some warm milk ready!" Bacas yells out to the bartender.

The bartender's eyebrows furrow, questioning the chief Enforcer with her eyes. The members of the gang all stare at their leader.

"Greyson looked like he was about to cry!" Bacas says.

The men in the casino erupt in laughter.

The voice of one of the twins rises above the rest. "What a baby! He needs to learn to keep his mouth shut. With a temper like that I am surprised he didn't pull out his blaster and point it at the stranger's face," he says.

The bartender puts a dirty glass on the bar and fills it with thin grey milk. "It should be warm by the time he gets back!"

"Bet he is on his way to cry into a pillow because Bacas told him to shut up!" the second twin says. Reenacting the scene for the rest of the men, he holds his breath until he is red in the face before he stands up, knocking down the chair behind him in the process. He stomps towards the front door. Fresh laughter fills the casino.

"Hey, guys, take it easy," the Operator says to the men.

The laughter trickles away. The men all look at the newest gang member, unsure of what to do with the statement.

"Maybe he really had to go to the bathroom," the Operator says, deadpan.

Bacas bursts out laughing. The rest of the men follow in their leader's footsteps.

"You know what?" Bacas says with a smile. He shakes his head and chuckles twice more. "You're a funny guy. I wasn't so sure about you. My men didn't trust you. Greyson definitely didn't trust you, still doesn't, I'm sure, but you are worth keeping around. Even if it's just for the laughs!" Bacas slaps the table in front of him.

"I do what I can," the Operator says. He lets himself crack a reserved smile, aware of how the tide has turned for Greyson and aware the tide could turn for him too. If he isn't careful he could find himself at the wrong end of the gang's jokes or, worse, at the wrong end of their guns.

"Grab the computer and come over here," Bacas says to the Operator as he pats the chair next to him. He leans over as the Operator sits down next to him. "Just so you know, Greyson knows how to hold a grudge," he says so only the Operator can hear. The men around them continue to howl with laughter.

"Noted," the Operator says.

Bacas adjusts the computer in front of him. "I want to double check some of the figures," he says.

The Operator pretends not to pay any attention as Bacas logs into the government system. He puts his hand down to his side and snaps his fingers. Fenix comes to his side and the Operator scratches the dog behind the ears. Occasional glances at the computer screen never linger long enough to read the words displayed. The men in the casino calm down. They drink and smoke while they wait for instructions from the chief Enforcer.

"You can take a look at what I'm doing," Bacas says. His eyes stay on the screen ahead of him.

The Operator feigns surprise. "Why would I care what you are doing?"

"Beats me, but don't pretend you haven't peeked at the screen a few times. If you want to see what the government wants me to do, scoot over and watch. Don't be shy about it."

The Operator shuffles his chair to the side and looks at the screen.

"Right now I am reporting the shipment as damaged in transit. Not exactly wrong, but they don't need to know about the theft."

The Operator leans back in his chair and looks at Bacas. "If it isn't reported as theft how will they know to use more protection next time?"

"They will know because I will tell the person in charge of shipment. It's a separate division and they can take care of it without a paper trail." Bacas taps the screen. "All these guys need to know is that we never received the Stim, so they can adjust our next shipment to include more."

Bacas stays focused on the computer while the Operator watches and pets Fenix.

"Since the attack happened so high up it isn't technically my problem. The upper levels know about our current situation with the Sisters and are hesitant to get themselves involved. They leave problems down here to me," Bacas says while he types. He has typed out a block of text large enough to take up most of the screen.

"Greyson usually does all this admin stuff," Bacas continues. He reads over the report and pushes send. He leans back and focuses on the Operator. "I just told them it was a mechanical failure and suggested that maybe the mechanics failed to perform the necessary checks to make sure the carrier was prepared to fly. Some jobs will probably be lost in the inspection station but no one I need will be affected."

"Do you have full access to the government database?" the Operator says.

"Yes."

"Could you find someone on the upper levels?"

"In theory, as long as they don't have someone hiding their file. Looking for someone in particular?"

"Could you look up," the Operator says. He pauses. "My sister?"

"Sure, what is her name?"

"Patrice. She was born on the fifty-second," the Operator says. His stomach contracts at the mention of her name.

It doesn't take long for Bacas to find a short list of women who fit the description. He clicks the top result. "This her?" Bacas says, pointing to a picture of Patrice on the screen.

"Yes," the Operator says. His heart skips a beat. She is beautiful, more beautiful than he remembers.

"She lives on the eighty-first," Bacas says.

She has made it even higher than the two of them had aimed when they were still together all those years ago. "Guess she does now," the Operator says.

"So. You have a sister on the eighty-first," Bacas says. He turns and looks at the Operator, his eyes wide. "There is a lot to learn about you, amigo. It seems we have all underestimated our newest comrade!"

"We don't speak anymore," he says, in an effort to downplay her significance. He turns away from the screen, ashamed and upset with himself. Not because they don't speak anymore—that was his choice—but because he has let her name escape his lips in a momentary lapse of judgement. He should have never told Bacas to search for her. Now the Enforcer knows more about his past than he is comfortable with.

"Sorry if it is a sore subject," Bacas says.

Fenix scratches the Operator's foot with his paw, a sign that he needs to be taken outside.

"If you don't need anything right now do you mind if I go meet with Miguel for lunch?" the Operator asks Bacas.

"Miguel? Who's Miguel?"

"The pool hall owner. It's a small place farther down the avenue. That's where I've been staying."

Bacas flashes a mischievous grin. "I assumed there was some woman you shared a bed with. Why the pool hall? We have better rooms for you here."

"My hovercraft broke down in front of the place and I stayed because Fenix likes it there. Don't you, buddy?" The Operator pats his friend on the head.

"I've learned a lot about you today! Go on, there's nothing to do until this evening. I'll see you then."

20

THE MIDLINERS

THE OPERATOR TAKES his time on his way to the station.

Fenix follows close behind him through the bazaar but, once they leave the crowds, the dog begins to walk ahead. He is able to sense they are headed back to the midline and looks back every block to make sure the Operator still follows. The dog stops to investigate a pile of trash surrounded by rats. A low growl is all it takes to scare the wild rats away, but the messenger rats don't pay attention to the dog's threats. Fenix, confused by their lack of response, decides to keep his distance instead of pressing the issue.

The Operator walks close to the buildings with an eye out for other members of the gang, ready to make it seem like he was sent to patrol the area. The Operator curses the haze. He can't see farther than a block ahead and he wants to be able to see if any of Bacas's men are at the entrance to the station. Two women surrounded by five young children materialize through the haze and walk past him on their way to the bazaar. The dog continues his relaxed walk with his head held high. The Operator is reassured by the dog's confidence. His own approach to the station is taken with slow, deliberate steps.

The street outside the station is empty. The Operator walks down the stairs and sees a rat scurry across the platform. At the bottom of the stairs, before he walks onto the platform, he looks around the side of the building and can see the rest of the station is deserted except for the rats. Fenix is still at the top of the stairs. The Operator looks at his companion and pats his thigh twice. The dog runs down the stairs and stands at the Operator's side, his tongue hanging out to the side.

There is movement in the darkness of the far tunnel. The Operator stays rooted to his spot and watches as a human crawls on all fours, their chest held upright, just inside the shadow. Fenix's nose quivers when the smell of the midliner reaches his nostrils. The dog lets out a low growl and the midliner on the rails stares at the staircase. The Operator steps onto the platform with his hands held in front of him. The midliner disappears down the tunnel in a flash.

The Operator takes off at a full sprint and, with Fenix close behind, runs the length of the platform. He jumps down from the ledge onto the rails. He plunges into the darkness of the tunnel but stops when he hears Fenix whimper behind him. Still on the platform, the dog paces back and forth and is unable to commit to the leap onto the rails.

"Come on, boy, you can do it!" the Operator urges. He is about to go back and grab Fenix from the ledge when the dog takes the leap. Fenix stumbles on the landing and, after a quick shake, runs to the Operator's side.

The two of them set off at a jog as they try to catch up to the midliner. Their eyes begin to adjust to the darkness of the tunnel.

Fenix runs ahead of the Operator when he catches the scent of the midliner. The dog turns left down a side tunnel and the Operator is able to follow with enough time to see the dog make a second left into another tunnel up ahead, a smaller tunnel designed for humans to walk through. The Operator chases his dog and, by extension, the midliner down a long corridor before he sees the dog disappear to the right.

"Fenix," the Operator calls out, worried about the distance between them. He whistles into the darkness. "Come back," he says.

The Operator turns down the tunnel on the right and comes face to face with two deformed humans, a male and a female. The male holds Fenix off the ground by the back of the neck while the dog struggles to get away. Both deformed humans sit in a squat with their hands on the ground and their heads tilted to the side while they inspect their captive. Their pale skin is visible through tattered clothes and both have long, dark hair that sits in matted strings on their heads. If the Operator had stumbled upon them when they were asleep he would have thought they were drowned corpses.

The Operator draws his blaster from its holster and points it at the two midliners. They recoil in horror but keep a firm hold on the dog. One of the two midliners, the female, wants to run but she refuses to leave her partner behind. The midliner who has a hold of Fenix can't run because he has lost the use of one of his hands.

"Get that thing out of our faces," the midliner who holds Fenix hisses at the Operator.

"Will you let go of the dog if I do?" the Operator says. It would be easy for him to take two quick shots and eliminate them, but he doesn't want to escalate the situation.

"A dog?" The two midliners look at Fenix in awe as he continues to struggle. "Never seen a dog before . . ." says the male midliner, his voice trailing off. For a moment they have forgotten about their fear of the blaster pointed at them.

"Thought is was a new kind of rat. It's scruffy," the female midliner says.

"Get a good look then let him go. I'll put my blaster away when you do."

"Don't even want a dog," the midliner who has a hold of Fenix says. He tosses Fenix towards the Operator and the dog lands in a heap. "We prefer rats. You can have him. Just get that thing out of our faces!" For a moment the Operator is worried the dog has a broken leg. The moment doesn't last long because Fenix bounces up, shakes himself off, and stands by the right leg of the Operator. He barks at the two midliners.

"Easy, buddy," the Operator says to the dog. He puts his blaster away and gives Fenix two quick pats on the dog's side, the whole time ready to draw his blaster again if he needs to.

"Why do your people love those things so much?" the female midliner says.

"They kill people," the male adds.

"Yes, they can." The Operator pauses to think. "We have them because we don't always get along."

"Things are different on the surface," the female midliner murmurs to her partner the same way a mother would explain a cultural difference to her child.

"Have you seen a blaster kill someone before?" the Operator asks. He wants to direct the conversation to Greyson's failed exchange.

"We haven't but Usryd has. He's still upset from what he witnessed three hungers ago," the male midliner says.

"Hasn't eaten since," adds the female.

"What did he see?" the Operator says.

"He watched somebody extinguish another's life. None of them were from the tunnels."

"There is no honor in killing another."

"He saw it? Could I talk to him?" the Operator says.

"Not now. He hasn't come back yet."

"Come back? From where?" the Operator asks.

"He risked the light to grab the metal that your people love so much. Once it was in his hand he was worried it would make him want to kill too, so he went to talk to the fish without eyes. Hasn't been back since."

"He has the metal?" the Operator says when he realizes "metal" is their term for the blaster.

"Yes." A shuffle behind the midliners pulls their attention away from the Operator.

"Could you take me to him?"

Neither midliner responds or gives any indication they heard the question. The Operator repeats himself and the male turns back around.

"Not now! We are supposed to be out finding rats for the next meal."

"How about you bring me the metal? I will get rid of it for you."

The female midliner turns around and looks at the Operator as if he has two heads. "We aren't touching it!" she says.

"Then take me to Usryd. I will take it from him," the Operator says.

"I told you, he hasn't come back yet. When he does we will tell him about your offer."

The sound of claws behind the two midliners, closer this time, makes them both turn around. They take off and chase after the sound.

The Operator and Fenix look at each other. "We will have to come back," the Operator says, disappointed. They head back in the direction they came. When the Operator thinks they are lost he allows Fenix to lead. The dog is able to get them back to the station within minutes. The Operator helps Fenix onto the platform before he climbs up himself.

"They have the weight of a hundred levels above them. No

wonder they walk around on all fours," the Operator says to Fenix with a look back into the darkness of the tunnel.

The dog looks at the Operator and wags his tail.

21

THE BRIEF

"How was lunch?" Bacas asks when the Operator returns with Fenix to Suerte. The computer is still open in front of him and scattered papers now cover the rest of the table. Empty dishes are stacked on the front edge of the other two round tables in the back of the casino. In the center of the middle table is a large tray filled with some sort of leftover casserole that must have been the group's lunch.

"It was good," the Operator says. His stomach reminds him he hasn't eaten since breakfast in the pool hall. "Did you already eat?" he says as he pulls out a chair and sits down opposite the chief Enforcer. Fenix lies on the ground by his feet.

"Not yet. I eat a late lunch," says Bacas. The dirty dishes must belong to the rest of the gang, the ones who eat on a schedule different from their leader.

"Why were you at the midline?" Bacas says. He shuts the computer and rests his elbows on the table.

The Operator blinks twice. "I went there to think," he says.

Bacas's eyes narrow with suspicion. "Nobody goes there with any sort of regularity unless they have business with the White Jackets. Have you been in contact with them?"

"You know the last time I talked to them; we went to meet them in the station right after. Remember?"

"I remember." Bacas's blue eyes focus on the Operator's face, looking for signs of a lie. "From now on, consider the station off-limits. Understood?"

"Understood," the Operator replies with a shrug.

"Glad we are on the same page. Look, I need you here before dawn tomorrow morning. Don't be late. Take the rest of today off," Bacas says. He opens the computer and resumes his work.

The Operator gets up from the table and makes his way to the front door. Across the room from Bacas, before he is able to leave, the Operator is stopped by two young men. One of them, the blond shadow always with Greyson, is tall, thin, and has whispers of a blond mustache on his youthful face. The other is stocky with flecks of grey in his beard. Both men were part of the group who surrounded and kicked the hovercraft with Greyson.

The stocky one gets closer and closer to the Operator until their faces are inches apart. "You think you're big stuff now, walking around here like you're untouchable. Bacas's new pet!" He looks the Operator up and down. "You don't seem so tough."

"Who would stop us from killing you right now?" the blond man says.

The man in front of the Operator forms his hand into the shape of a gun and puts it to the Operator's temple. "We could make it quick." His hand moves down and is shoved into the Operator's gut. "Or we could drag it out," he says.

"We would take *good* care of you," the blond says. "First your kneecaps, then your ankles, then your elbows. A nice six-pack to begin the longest night of your life."

The Operator doesn't move a muscle. He doesn't even blink. The silence makes the two men uncomfortable.

"What do you have to say about all that?" the stocky man says.

"Are you done?" the Operator says. His attention is directed to the blond. "You're the one who follows Greyson around like a dog. What's your name?"

"Ludavico," the blond man replies.

"And you are?" he says to the man in front of his face.

"Manolo."

"Good to know. Bacas said I have the afternoon to myself. I don't really feel like taking out the trash for him but if the two of you don't stop talking I will be happy to help him out."

The blond man pulls his blaster out and points it at the Operator's head. "You have a death wish, stranger?" Ludavico says. The tip of the blaster digs into the middle of the Operator's forehead.

The Operator strains his neck against the force to make sure his head doesn't move.

"Not in here, Bacas will have you killed," Manolo says to his friend as he wraps his fingers around the muzzle of the blaster.

The end of the blaster stays in place for a while longer while Ludavico decides his next move. He pulls the blaster away in frustration and storms farther into Suerte.

"Watch your back, stranger. We have our eyes on you," Manolo says.

THE OPERATOR MAKES sure he is on the way to the casino well before the sun comes up the next day. The ground is still wet from rain that fell while he slept. Without any idea about what Bacas wants him to do, he decided it was best to leave Fenix with Miguel at the pool hall. He turns the corner and sees the glow from the bright lights of the sign above Suerte. Through the haze he can see two men approach the casino from the other side of the street. The Operator meets Manolo and Ludavico at the front door.

"What are you doing here?" Ludavico snarls.

"Bacas told me to be here at dawn," the Operator says.

The two men look at each other, annoyed with the new development. "Any idea what he wants us to do this early in the morning?" Manolo asks.

"None. I just do what I'm told," the Operator says.

Two more men walk up from behind the Operator. The twins. They argue with each other as they approach.

"I'm telling you, the rats have become smarter because of the training from humans," one of the twins says to the other.

The three men already at the casino are silent as the argument unfolds.

"Listen. Everyone knows rats have always been smart. Humans just taught them a new skill."

The first twin rolls his eyes. "How could they have been this smart before? Impossible. You see the wild rats these days? They know to open latches to get into the trash. It's because they are smarter than before."

"The rats have always been able to do that, you just don't remember!"

"My memory is just fine, it is your memory that needs help. Maybe we can get a human to train you to make you smarter."

Both twins ball their hands into fists and stare at each other. It's impossible to tell them apart.

Manolo walks up to the twins and pats each of them on the shoulder at the same time. "We all know you never fight, so stop pretending you will," he says.

"If he keeps making fun of my memory we will!" one twin says.

Manolo laughs out loud. "All right, tough guys. Let it go this time. We have a job to do." He turns to the Operator. "Stranger, this is Dig and Doug. Nobody can tell them apart."

The door opens behind the five men before another word can be said. Inside is Greyson, eyes bloodshot and hair disheveled. Even Ludavico is surprised to see him there. Greyson looks at the Operator with hostile eyes. The Operator ignores the unspoken threat and pushes his way past Greyson.

"Where's Bacas?" Manolo asks Greyson after a quick glance to the empty back-corner table.

"Upstairs," Greyson says. He leads the five men to the bar, where a manila folder waits on the counter. Greyson picks up the folder. "We need you guys to kill an Enforcer in Sigma District. He's in charge of levels four to ten. The government has been trying to get rid of him through legal means but he knows how to work the system."

"Why don't they just send a squad to kill him?" says Ludavico.

"They are," says Greyson.

All five men look at Greyson with confusion in their eyes.

Greyson stares at the men in front of him. "Seriously, guys? You're the squad."

"I knew that," says a twin, Doug or Dig.

"No you didn't," says the other twin.

"Yes I did!"

"Prove it! You had no idea, just like the rest of us!"

"Will you two shut up!" says Greyson.

The twins both shut their mouths.

"You five are responsible for killing the Enforcer. From what we know, there are four android security guards. Four androids, five of you. Worst-case scenario, we lose four of you and the fifth can still take him out. Just make sure you kill an android before you get killed and the numbers work out."

"The Enforcer has to know how to use a blaster," Manolo says.

"Technically, yes. But based on the record from his blaster he hasn't shot in over two years. We doubt he has shot any other weapons, so let's just say it's been a while. Be quick with the trigger and you should be fine."

"His blaster tracks when it was last shot . . ." the Operator says to himself, remembering his discussion with Klepsydra.

"Yes, all government-issued blasters keep track," Greyson says. His eyes become unfocused as he tries to recall a memory.

The Operator can guess what's on Greyson's mind.

"Sounds easy enough. What about the androids. Should we be worried about them?" Ludavico says.

The question brings Greyson back to the present moment. "Not too worried. These androids aren't the new ones we've been hearing about, those are all above the fiftieth. These are the older models. Their decisions take longer. Attack without hesitation and you should be fine."

The Operator thinks back to the android he once knew above the fiftieth. She must've been a newer model. Maybe the newest model.

"We know the four of you are quick with your blasters," Greyson says as he opens the folder and distributes security badges and contact lenses to the group. The men put the contacts in their eyes and the blue disappears. "The stranger here needs to be tested; we have no idea how good he is. If he dies," Greyson looks at the Operator and shrugs, "oh well."

Greyson walks behind the bar and pulls out a box from below the counter. He hands out two finger-sized vials to each man. "Take a Stim now to prime your nervous systems. Then, when you get outside the Enforcer's door, take the second to flood your systems. You won't be able to miss."

The other four men smile as they look at the two vials in their hands.

"Last question," Ludavico says. "Why so early? The sun isn't even up."

"This guy stays up all night drinking Sigma's version of Serum. The harsh stuff, not even close to the quality we get from the Sisters. The kind that'll knock you out. According to our reports, he usually goes to bed," Greyson looks at his watch, "about an hour ago. He should be asleep for at least another four. By the time anybody misses him you will already be back in Gamma."

The men roll up their sleeves and stick the vial against their forearms. The Operator covers the vial with his hand and puts the wrong side against his skin on purpose so the others don't see he doesn't use. He isn't afraid of what could happen if he doesn't enhance his natural abilities because his life has already been taken from him once before. Death can't be any worse than the badlands.

22

THE TRIP

FOUR OUT OF five men have a laser focus that can't be broken when the assassins leave Greyson and the casino behind. A fight right outside of Suerte is ignored on their way to the bazaar and the Operator isn't going to be the one to stop. Ludavico and Manolo lead the group together up front, the twins walk side by side in the middle, and the Operator brings up the rear. Ludavico and Manolo shove aside everyone in their way as they walk through the bazaar and turn towards the station. Free from the crowds in the intersection, the two pairs of men in front of the Operator all break out into a steady jog. The Operator doesn't expect the change in their pace and he has to tie his duster around his waist to keep it from flapping behind him as he struggles to keep up. It doesn't seem right for him to be on this mission without Fenix but there is no way the dog could have come.

The men jog down the steps into the station. Ludavico and Manolo take every step on the way down while the twins, in unison, take every other. The Operator holds onto the side rail and takes each step on the way down. The men ahead of him stop on the platform and inspect the station.

"We need to cross the midline?" the Operator says while trying to hide how out of breath he is.

Manolo looks at him, his wind unaffected, his eyes curious. "No," he says.

"Jacket's making me hot," he says to Manolo to explain his heavy breathing. Other than the focus in their eyes the other four men don't look any different than when they were in Suerte. The Operator wouldn't have believed they jogged to the station if he wasn't behind them when they did.

Out of nowhere the men all jump onto the rails and turn towards the left tunnel.

"We have to go in the tunnels?" the Operator asks. He wonders if the midliners down the tunnel on the right ever communicate with their counterparts on the left.

"This is the only way to get to Sigma," Manolo says, as if this fact is known to everyone.

"All of the ways on the ground are blocked off," Dig or Doug adds.

"You aren't worried about midliners?" the Operator asks.

"You sound like Greyson," Manolo says. "They make sure to keep their distance. They know what will happen if they don't."

"We will shoot them," one of the twins says. He pulls out his blaster and shoots a rat off the rail as it crawls past. The rat explodes in a puddle of guts and gore.

"Good shot," the Operator says.

"Don't flatter him, it's the Stim," says Ludavico.

"I can shoot that well with or without the Stim," the twin says to Ludavico.

The other twin looks at him with disbelief. "You're crazy! You are a terrible shot without Stim," he says to his brother.

The twin who took the shot punches his brother on the arm. "Like you're any better!"

"I'll beat you senseless," the twin who was punched says.

"You're a terrible shot and you know it!" He balls his hand into a fist and prepares to lunge. Ludavico grabs him before he can strike and Manolo holds the other.

"Enough!" Manolo screams. "No more arguing until we get back! Last thing we need is you two clowns drawing attention to us when we are in Sigma."

"Shall we?" the Operator says.

The twins both look at their watches. "We have to wait until the top of the hour. Two minutes left."

"Midliners always run and hide at the top of the hour," Dig or Doug adds.

The Operator laughs. After his encounter with the two midliners yesterday he doesn't believe they even know whether it's day or night, let alone when the hour switches over. "How do you know that?"

"Everyone knows that. They scatter and hide, so we go through the tunnels at the top of the hour."

Ludavico looks at the twins, annoyed. "They will scatter ahead of us no matter what time we go through the tunnels. They want nothing to do with us. We wait for the top of the hour because Bacas tells us to."

The Operator has his wind back and walks towards the tunnel. He tries to see through the darkness but is unable to see farther than what is illuminated by the light from the station. He turns back to the group. Manolo has his eyes on his watch and bobs his head as each second passes. He lifts his head up and walks into the darkness of the tunnel.

"Follow me," he says before he takes off at a run.

The men run single file through the darkness. Ludavico is behind Manolo, the twins are behind Ludavico, and again the Operator brings up the rear. They run for what seems to the Operator like an eternity. He has trouble with the pace the stimmed men set, but he knows that he can't ask them to take a break or even to slow down. He reaches into his pocket and feels the vial of Stim as he runs. It has been a long time since he has used and he doesn't want to break his streak now.

He counts five more steps. Once. Twice. Ten times. His ability to hold on fades fast. Fifteen iterations of five more steps. Sixteen. He won't make it to the twentieth cycle. Just five more steps. Has he counted five more steps twenty-five times or twenty-six now? He can't be sure. He takes the lid off the Stim in his pocket. Just before he stabs himself in the thigh through his pants, light shines ahead in the distance.

The count ends at thirty-one iterations of five more steps. The group stops to inspect the station before they walk into the light. Nobody in sight. None of the group notices when the Operator doubles over to catch his breath.

They walk through the station and up a flight of stairs onto the streets of Sigma district. If the Operator hadn't known about their trip through the tunnel he would guess they are still in Gamma.

"Keep your mouths shut," Manolo says. At first the Operator thinks he has issued a reminder to the twins not to argue, but then he remembers that, according to Miguel, the people in this district all have pointed teeth.

"And walk," says Ludavico. Nothing more suspicious than a group of unknown men who jog through the streets, a dead give-away they are stimmed.

The other members of the group have a hard time at such a slow pace and have to find ways to deal with the suppressed energy. Manolo clenches and unclenches his fists, Ludavico doesn't stop blinking. The twins both deal with their extra energy in the same way: by biting the space between their thumb and forefinger on their right hands. One of the twins' hands is separated from his mouth long enough for the Operator to see the chewed-up flesh, and he's surprised the hand isn't bleeding.

The Operator catches his breath while they walk. Thoughts about the upcoming climb to the higher levels begins to affect his nerves. A smoky image of Patrice has already begun to form in the back corner of his mind and he works hard to make sure her edges don't solidify.

23

THE ASCENT

Manolo stops the group in front of a building that has been consumed by fire up to the third floor. The structure is still able to stand even without a solid base of support. The numerous walkways connecting it to the surrounding buildings serve as braces, the arms of its neighbors not letting their comrade fall victim to gravity.

"He lives on the tenth level of that building over there," Manolo says, with a finger pointed across the street. "We have someone who will make sure we get onto the tenth level in this building," he says as he points to the fire-damaged building in front of them. "Once we are up there, we will use that catwalk to cross into the building where the Enforcer lives." The men all look at the covered walkway pointed to by Manolo. "There will be security guards but the passes Greyson gave us will get us through."

"Android security?" Dig or Doug asks.

"Not entirely sure but they *should* be human. They don't work for the Enforcement Division, they work for surveillance. Surveillance can't afford androids this low."

Both twins nod, as if they already knew this fact but didn't remember.

Manolo continues, "Once we get into this building we make our way to his apartment. That's where the android security will be. We get past them and make our way to the Enforcer, who should still be asleep."

"Easy target and a quick kill," Ludavico says.

"Exactly," says Manolo with a nod. "Then we go back. Understood?" He looks at the Operator.

"Seems straightforward enough," the Operator says.

The other members nod and they all enter the burned-out building.

Black soot covers the walls inside. There is a stairwell that the Operator can't believe can support the weight of one man, let alone five. On the first-floor landing the Operator thinks he sees a pair of eyes peer from the darkness at the end of the hallway but they disappear before the sight can register in his mind, so he can't be sure.

A loud crack and the step under Ludavico buckles. Ludavico holds onto the side rails and stops to see if the step will separate from the rest. The stair stays in place, with a large crack down the center. "Watch out for this one," Ludavico says.

Thoughts of Patrice float through the Operator's mind as the group climbs higher and higher in the burned-out building. He hasn't been this high up in a long time, and each step he takes brings him closer to her. Being this close makes him worried he will see her again even though there is no way she would be anywhere close to such low levels. Maybe he doesn't want her to see him.

The stairwell ends on the fourth floor and they exit into a hallway. The character of the building changes once they step through the door. No longer burned-out, the hallways are covered with old grey carpet stained from years of use. Graffiti covers the walls but the structure seems much more solid. The feeling that the structure could shift at any moment persists.

Arrows direct the group to another set of stairs down the hall. Manolo opens the door and a nest of cockroaches scurry into the walls to escape the light. No stairs lead down, only up. The people above the fourth level like to pretend there is no world below the reclaimers and never use the stairs that could lead them down to the ground level. The group climbs again.

"We could take these all the way up to the hundredth but we could never leave the stairwell," Ludavico says.

The Operator is surprised to hear this. Even with so much of his life spent in the higher levels, he didn't know the stairwell could be taken between them, and he suspects most of the others who live so high don't know either. Everyone passes between levels by vertical transport, a modified elevator that hovers between buildings, able to be ordered like a taxi.

"Have you ever been up that high?" the Operator asks Ludavico.

"I've made my way to the sixtieth before I decided to come back down. Walking up so many steps got boring after a while since I knew I couldn't leave the stairwell."

"Did you even try?" Dig or Doug asks as they climb.

"No. What was the point? Up there they use biometric sensors. The doors can tell if you are supposed to be there and they will unlock for you. The door on sixty was locked so I just came back down," Ludavico says. His voice has a hint of nostalgia. It could also be remorse.

"I bet I could figure out a way to get past those doors," Dig or Doug says.

His twin looks at him and rolls his eyes. "Do you say dumb stuff to hear yourself talk, or do you actually believe what comes out of your mouth?"

Manolo looks back at the two of them from the seventh-floor

landing. "Don't even start. In fact, one of you come up here with me, the other can go back with Ludavico. You," he points to the Operator, "walk in the middle."

They rearrange themselves and continue to the tenth level. Manolo stands outside the door and waits for the rest of the group to stand with him. Three knocks, three pauses, two knocks, two pauses, and one knock. The door opens, and the group stands in front of a tall person in a black mask. The black-masked person is thin and could be a man or woman.

"Bacas said there would be four," the person says. The mask has a voice changer installed.

"Bacas forgot to count me," Manolo replies. "He meant four in addition to me."

There is a pause as the masked human weighs the words and decides what to do. This space in time would be when an android would analyze data and calculate probabilities, if this were an android.

Manolo doesn't falter and stands with certainty.

"Tell him to be more careful next time," the person says.

They walk through the door onto the tenth level. No graffiti covers the walls, and the carpet isn't stained. The group passes by a security guard and marches onto the walkway between buildings. The guard nods in recognition but doesn't ask for their badges. His job is to make sure people that shouldn't be there don't enter; he doesn't care who leaves.

A lethargic security guard at the other end of the walkway stands up to block their path. "Passes," he says. His pointed teeth are stained brown and he smells like he has never heard of a shower. The five of them have their credentials scanned and are waved through.

The Operator looks down at his pass once they are in the Enforcer's building. Somehow he ended up with Ludavico's pass and the guard didn't notice.

"Here, this is yours," the Operator says. He hands the pass to Ludavico. "Do you have mine?"

Ludavico pulls his own pass from his pocket and takes a look. "Nope, I have one of the twins'." He turns to Dig and Doug and hands them the pass. "This belongs to one of you two."

"Do either of you have mine?" the Operator says.

"Here," Dig or Doug says. He hands the Operator his badge.

Manolo has turned around and watches the badge exchange with anger in his eyes. "Everyone needs to be more careful! This shouldn't happen," he says. He pauses after a look at the twins. "Except for the two of them. Nobody can tell them apart anyways. But you two could've gotten us caught!"

Ludavico pockets the correct badge. "Blame Greyson, he handed them to us. Besides, the guard didn't even notice. He only cared that they scanned."

Manolo looks at the blond. "We might not always be so lucky. You of all people should appreciate that fact."

Ludavico is thrust into his own head, into his own memories, and stares at the floor.

The group begins to walk down a curved hall. There are a hundred steps between each door. "These places must be huge," Ludavico says. "Do you think people live in each one?"

"Some of them are companies, but yes, people live in most of them," Manolo says. "Some families prefer to stay on the tenth level with a lot of space instead of going up a level or two. The Enforcer stays here because he is in charge of the fourth through the tenth."

The Operator has no idea how Manolo knows so much about life on the tenth. Maybe he came from a higher level too. Was Manolo born higher than him? The Operator shakes his head, annoyed the thought crossed his mind.

"Which one is his?" Dig or Doug asks.

"It's coming up," Manolo says.

The group passes three more doors and stops outside one made of stainless steel.

"All right, everyone, game time. Blasters ready?" Manolo says.

"Yes," says Ludavico.

"Yes," says the Operator.

"Ready," say the twins at the same time.

"Take your second Stim," Manolo orders. He pulls his own vial from his pocket and the group follows his lead. The Operator pulls the vial from his pocket and pretends to inject himself in the forearm for a second time.

Manolo knocks on the door. Three knocks, three pauses. Then another pause. Another. After the seventh pause, the door opens. A grey-haired lady with tiny glasses squints at the five men in front of her.

"Can I help you?" she says with a delicate voice before the blasters the men have drawn can register. Once they do, her eyes begin to flutter left to right, independent of each other.

Dig or Doug puts his blaster to her head and fires.

"Nope, you've been great," the twin says as the woman's head explodes. Circuitry flies through the air.

The five men rush into the apartment.

24

THE ANDROIDS

Bacas's men walk over the headless android and find themselves in a wide, open room. No walls separate the space, but the furniture is arranged so the purpose of each area is clear. The kitchen on their left has an island with stools around it, and across the room, couches mark the living room. The Operator could drive his hovercraft through the open spaces between sections if he could ever get the vehicle inside. The men all look at each other, confused about the lack of android security they were told would be present.

A corridor on the right side of the room shares a wall with the curved hall outside the metal door. Without a word to the rest of the group, the Operator peels off to investigate. The end is out of view behind the left curvature of the corridor, and the Operator wonders if whatever is behind the wall on his left is a part of this apartment or another. Ten steps in, he realizes that if there are any androids in the unseen end of the corridor there is no cover for him in the event of a shoot-out. He makes sure his finger is ready on the trigger.

A window covered with steel bars is at the end of the corridor. Outside the window is a metal staircase.

The sound of blaster fire reaches him from around the bend, followed by a large crash. He jogs back to rejoin his team and stops to survey the scene before he enters the main room. The other members of his team have taken cover behind the island counter in the kitchen. Ludavico lies on the floor in a heap. The other three have their backs to the counter, and when they see the Operator, they nod their heads towards the rest of the open space.

The Operator crouches down and peeks around the corner. Seven androids fire constant shots at the counter, intent on shooting through the protection to their quarry on the other side. They are all the same model, identical seven-foot-tall men.

The Operator turns back, faces the wall opposite him, and stands up. He takes a big breath and follows with a slow exhale. With the position of each android in his mind's eye, he maps out the seven shots it will take to eliminate each. After some quick calculations, he knows he won't be able to eliminate the seventh android before it is able to process his position.

Six shots and drop, shoot the seventh from the floor.

Another deliberate inhale and he turns the corner.

Three heads explode from three well-placed shots and electrical parts fly through the air. The Operator lines up the fourth and fifth and is about to fire when he realizes the sixth android has taken a step forward and now blocks the seventh android from view. His fourth shot finds a fourth android head and the fifth does the same. The Operator deviates from his original plan of six straight headshots and shoots the sixth android in the knee. The android loses its balance and drops to the floor.

The seventh android has processed the development of another team member and, with the sixth android down, has a clear shot at the Operator. The Operator sticks to his original plan for the seventh and is already on his way to the floor as he fires. Another android head explodes at the same moment the Operator hits the floor.

The sixth android has his blaster aimed on the Operator as he tries to regain his footing. He gets up, falls, and tries to get up again, unaware that his leg is useless without its major joint but unable to perform any other task. The Operator rolls out of the way, grateful the android has been caught in a loop. His plan didn't account for the sixth android to change his position.

"Look at this guy," says Dig or Doug as he stands up from behind the counter. He walks up to the android and taps the android on the cheek a few times.

"It'll be over soon," the twin says.

The android continues to try to stand up and falls down every time. His human face, with its pointed teeth, is directed at the spot where the Operator had been moments before. The only part of the android that is able to move outside the loop is his eyes. The android focuses on each member of the group in turn but never moves his blaster from the spot where the Operator once stood.

Manolo walks up to the android, puts his blaster into his mouth, and pulls the trigger. Sparks fly from exposed wires as the last android head is sent into oblivion. The android falls to the ground.

"Where did you learn to shoot like that?" Manolo asks the Operator with a mixture of awe and anger.

"You might be a better shot than Bacas," Dig or Doug says.

"No way he's better than Bacas. It's the Stim. Bacas can shoot like that without it," the other twin says.

"There's no way to say for sure," the first twin says. "Besides, I didn't say he was, I said he might be. Don't be so dense."

"I've seen Bacas do something like this on Stim but never dry. I would be curious to see who is better. Does he know how good you are with a blaster?" Manolo asks the Operator, less upset than he was just a moment ago.

"I don't see how he could know; there hasn't been anything to shoot. Unless you count all the rats," the Operator replies.

"Was the bedroom down the hall?" Manolo asks.

"No, there's just a window at the end," the Operator says.

"Then let's find the bedroom and kill this guy so we can get out of here," one twin says.

The men find a staircase tucked away behind the left wall on the far side of the room.

"Should we just leave Ludavico like that?" the Operator says.

"We will grab him on the way out," Manolo says.

The twins follow Manolo up the stairs, with the Operator behind them. At the top of the stairs is another space, as large as the one below, with a bed in the far corner above the entrance to the apartment. No other furniture is in the room, but empty bottles litter the floor. The light that spills in from the staircase is enough for the group to see the Enforcer they were sent to kill asleep on the bed.

The men surround the man—Manolo on one side, the twins on the other, and the Operator at the foot of the bed. The Enforcer is asleep on his stomach. Manolo looks at the rest of his team and aims his blaster at the back of the Enforcer's head.

The man turns over in his sleep and the group stares at Bacas. He is clean-shaven and, even in the soft glow of what little light reaches the bedroom, he looks less worn-out than the Bacas the group is used to taking orders from. The men don't know what to do. Dig and Doug both look at Manolo with mouths open. The man who they have been sent to kill is the same man who sent them.

The Operator is the only one who is able to organize his thoughts about the new development. If this is the real, human

Bacas, then the Bacas he takes orders from could be one of three things. One, they could be twins and the Bacas he knows wants to be the only one left alive because of some unresolved resentment the man has towards his brother. Two, the Bacas he knows could have altered his face at some point in the past to look like this man. Or three, the most interesting option to the Operator, the Bacas he knows is an android and this is the real thing.

While the rest of the group stands around, indecisive, the Operator pulls out his blaster and shoots the sleeping man in the heart. His eyes bolt open and stare at the ceiling as his life soaks the sheets beneath him. His gaze drops to the foot of the bed and he stares at the Operator, unaware of the other three members of the group. The two men lock eyes until the last of the Enforcer's life escapes him. With the Enforcer expired, the Operator looks up and sees the other three men staring at him with their mouths open.

25

THE ASSASSINATION

"WHAT? Bacas told us to kill the guy," the Operator says.

"But it *was* Bacas," Dig or Doug says.

"No, Bacas is back in Gamma," the Operator says. "Besides, if he wanted himself killed, who are we to question orders?"

"You have been holding out on us, stranger. With a man like you by our side, we could wipe the White Jackets from the earth in one night!" says Manolo.

The Operator ignores Manolo, walks back downstairs, and checks Ludavico's vitals. Blood stains the passed-out man's blond hair from where a piece of concrete ceiling fell and struck his head.

"He's all right for now, but he's lost a lot of blood," Manolo says from behind the Operator. "We need to get him back. Dig, Doug, take a third Stim and carry him back."

"A third in one day? Two is the most either of us has taken," one of the twins says. His twin nods in agreement.

"Don't worry, I've taken four before. Ludavico has taken five because . . . well, you know he has a death wish sometimes. He had to run for twelve hours straight then couldn't sleep for three days, but he lived."

"Barely," the Operator says as he looks down at the blond.

"Take the Stim and let's go!" Manolo commands the twins.

Dig and Doug each pull a vial from their pockets. They roll up their sleeves with identical movements and look at each other. They exchange a silent count to three before they both slam the vial into their arms. Their eyes get wide and their pupils dilate.

"Let's do this," the twins say at the same time. They throw Ludavico onto their shoulders in one swift motion.

"You got the legs on purpose. You didn't want to do the extra work!" Dig or Doug says.

"No I didn't! You grabbed his torso, it's your own fault."

Manolo interjects. "Switch when you get tired."

"I don't get tired," the twin who holds Ludavico's torso says. "I could carry him back myself if I had to!"

"I would love to see that. You couldn't carry him halfway without me," says his twin.

The four men walk out the front door with Ludavico in tow.

"I don't care how much you two argue as long as you get Ludavico back," Manolo says.

The Operator is the last one through the front door. He looks down the curved hall, past the twins, past Manolo, and sees the first of what turns out to be a group of people headed in their direction at a full sprint, blasters drawn. Reinforcements.

The Operator jumps in front of the men and ushers them back into the apartment. The other members of the group see the reinforcements just before the first blaster shot flies past Manolo's head.

Manolo's hands are on the side of his head as he paces from side to side back inside the apartment. "Where do we go?" he says. Shoulders begin to pummel the door from the outside.

"We can shoot our way through! We just stimmed, we can't miss!" Dig or Doug says.

"There are too many. Besides, if anyone is going to blast their way through, you know it will be him," Manolo says, with a gesture of his thumb towards the Operator.

"There's another way out down the corridor. It leads to a window and a metal staircase," the Operator tells the group.

"Then what are we waiting for?" Manolo yells.

The Operator looks for something heavy to place in front of the door. The sofa on the far side of the room is too far away to be dragged over in time.

"Hurry!" Manolo says from the corridor. The twins run ahead of him as fast as they can with Ludavico on their shoulders. The Operator follows them until they reach the window. The door slams open from the main room.

Manolo pulls open the metal grate but the window is stuck. The Operator tries to help but, even with the strength of the two men, the window won't budge.

"There has to be a trick to it!" Manolo whispers. Footsteps reach the men's ears from the reinforcements as they stream into the apartment.

The Operator takes a step back and looks at the window. He begins with the latches in the middle. His eyes fall to where the window meets the wall, then up the sides. On the right side, he sees a wing nut that seems out of place. He reaches up and unscrews the nut. A metal rod, with a hinge at the site of the nut, bends in half and falls to the ground. The metal clang bounces off the walls around them.

"If they didn't know where we were before they do now!" Manolo says.

"Get that window open!" the twins scream.

The window flies open with a yank from the Operator.

Footsteps echo from the far end of the corridor. Manolo climbs through the window and helps the twins get Ludavico through. The second twin climbs through just before a blaster shot hits the window where his head had been a moment before.

The Operator turns around to face the reinforcements. He sends the head of the closest android into oblivion and the body collapses to the floor in a heap.

"Go!" the Operator yells to the men on the other side. He takes the heads off of two more androids before he finds a sliver of time to get himself through the window. He turns back around, kneels on the metal staircase, and rests his blaster on the windowsill. The twins clamor down the staircase as they descend with their friend on their backs.

Manolo lingers for a moment before the Operator urges him to go on. "I will catch up," he says.

Two shots from the end of his blaster and two more bodies join the pile in the corridor. Four more androids run towards him with at least a dozen more a short distance behind them. He fires off four quick shots, each one finding the kneecap of the front four androids. All four of them stumble, and two of them get stuck in the feedback loop. The other two are able to raise their weapons and fire at the Operator but miss their target.

The Operator wasn't prepared to deal with newer models. Time to run. He clears two and three steps at a time on his way down. He catches up to the group as they pass Ludavico down to the roof of a lower building. Android footsteps on the metal staircase ring out as the pursuers gain ground.

"Hurry!" Manolo yells to one of the twins from the rooftop below. Dig or Doug drops their limp comrade the rest of the way down to where his twin and Manolo wait on the roof with outstretched arms. The twin and the Operator jump down at the same time and resume their escape. At the far end of the roof, the group looks down on a walkway a short drop below them that spans between their building and another. A window on the other end of the walkway is their only hope.

The men get onto the walkway with Ludavico and the Operator turns around to see the location of the androids behind them. Some of them are about to jump down onto the roof. He takes out the first three androids before he turns around and leaps onto the walkway. The group scrambles across and rushes through the window on the far side.

The Operator dives through and kneels on the carpet inside the building. Shots pass through the window and bury themselves in the wall behind him. He begins to take out androids as they spill over the edge of the roof onto the walkway. Two of them are shot midleap and hit the walkway at a strange angle before they tumble down to the ground. After he eliminates the first dozen androids he waits a moment to see if any more will show up. When there are none, he turns into the building to catch up with the other men in his group.

"That should be all of them," he tells Manolo when they are together again.

"For now. Those were on the district's network. Others will know where to go and will be on their way shortly. Sigma will pour androids over our heads until we drown," Manolo says.

The group runs through the hall and down a set of stairs. When the Operator begins to run out of breath he thinks about the Stim in his pocket and reminds himself he doesn't need it.

"We have to be close to ground level," Manolo says.

"Haven't been keeping track," one of the twins grunts.

"Neither have I," says the other. Both of their faces are bright red.

The group leaves the staircase and begins to run down another hallway.

Manolo studies the walls around them. "I think this is the building that was in a fire, except we came in from another side," he says. He runs up ahead and sticks his head through a door that hangs on loose hinges. "This way!" he yells before he disappears through the door.

The rest of the men follow Manolo's lead and find themselves in the same burned-out building from before. They descend the staircase and make sure to skip the broken step. They get to the ground level and begin to jog back to the station. They don't care if anybody from Sigma notices them. Even if they are noticed, the group will be long gone before authorities can investigate.

They are on the rails when the twins speak out. "We can't carry him much longer," one of them says.

"You two take him," says the other twin. "You can walk while we make sure no androids come from behind."

"No way. I've seen your dry shots, we're screwed if anything happens," Manolo says.

"I'll take him," the Operator says.

"It's a two-man job," the twins say in unison.

"I won't be able to jog, but I can walk with him. Here," he places his head under the hip of Ludavico and relieves the twins of their load. The Operator begins to march into the tunnel with the limp body in a fireman's carry position.

"Let's not make this too long. After seeing your skills with a blaster I would rather you watch our backs," Manolo says.

"Do the androids ever come in here?" one of the twins says. He leans back with his hands on his hips to stretch out.

"Why wouldn't they?" his brother says.

"Because there are no sensors down here and they would have no way to know where one district ends and the other begins. Whoever owns them wouldn't want to lose them," Dig or Doug says.

"How would they lose them?" the Operator says. He thinks back to the unclaimed androids from Sigma in the pool hall.

"They could be hacked. Nobody can afford androids this far

down, so whenever one shows up it's usually stolen," Manolo says.

"Let's hope they are programmed to stay out of the midline altogether," the Operator says. The words cause the body on his back to shift and he almost drops the unconscious Ludavico.

"Focus on your breathing and take one step at a time," Manolo says.

The Operator keeps his head down and squints to see where he places each footstep as he marches forward in the darkness with Ludavico on his back. Out of the corner of his eye he thinks he sees a pair of human eyes, at waist height, but when he turns to look the eyes disappear. The other four members of the group all walk backwards or sideways with their eyes focused on the circle of light from the station in case androids follow them into the tunnels. The Operator is the only one who is worried about the android they must report to when they get back to Gamma.

26

THE REPORT

THE GROUP REACHES the station in Gamma District without being attacked. The Operator sets Ludavico's body on the platform ledge and doubles over, hands on his knees. The other three men climb onto the ledge and the twins each offer a hand to the Operator.

"Give me a moment," he says.

"The tunnel didn't seem as long on the way there. The Stim made the time fly by," Manolo says. He rolls over his unconscious friend and inspects his head. "I don't think his skull is fractured," he says.

The Operator gestures for the twins to help him onto the platform. With their help he climbs up and twists to stretch out his back. He leans over to grab Ludavico and take him back to Suerte when he is stopped by a hand on his arm.

"Leave him for now. We'll go back to Suerte and send two more men to carry him the rest of the way. The twins can wait with him."

The casino quiets when Manolo and the Operator walk through the front door. Blue eyes all stare with curiosity as the two men walk to Bacas's table in the back corner. Their leader is seated at the table and rolls a single blue poker chip across the backs of his fingers, lost in thought. He looks up when he realizes the two men are in front of him.

"Where are the others?" he says.

"The twins are with Ludavico in the station. He's unconscious. We need two men to bring him back," Manolo says.

Bacas looks at two men at the bar and points with his chin towards the door. The two men set their drinks down without a word and leave.

"I've heard you've had an interesting day," Bacas says.

"We have."

"The whole city has heard. News of an Enforcer's murder spreads like wildfire. Of course, as an Enforcer myself, they expect me to help find whoever is responsible." He watches the blue chip crawl across his knuckles. "Were reinforcements dispatched?" he asks Manolo.

"More than I have ever seen. They were coming out of the woodwork," Manolo says.

"Makes sense, he has ten levels' worth of help below him."

"Greyson failed to mention that," the Operator says. He is surprised at how hoarse his voice is.

"How did he do?" Bacas asks Manolo, in reference to the Operator.

"Him?" Manolo points to the Operator with his thumb. "Honestly, we wouldn't have made it out alive if it wasn't for him. The things he can do with his blaster . . . Bacas, I haven't seen anything like it in a long time."

Bacas's ears perk up like a dog when he hears these words. "That good, huh? Better than you and Ludavico?"

"Much better, and it's not even close."

The sound of a glass slamming down comes from the bar. The two men in front of Bacas turn around and watch Greyson storm out.

"One of these days he will learn to control himself," Bacas says with sadness. "Go talk to him when we are done here," he says to Manolo.

Manolo nods.

"What happened to Ludavico?" Bacas says.

"He was hit by a piece of concrete. Knocked him out cold. He still hasn't woken up."

"Did you try and stim him awake?"

"We did when we were pinned down but it didn't work. The twins carried him back to the station in Sigma and he carried him through the tunnel."

"Alone?"

"Yes, sir," says Manolo.

Bacas looks at the Operator, impressed. The Operator wonders if the android is programmed to show emotions or if he learned how to display them over time.

"So you all made it back with security hot on your tails while carrying 'Vico?"

"Like I said, only because of him. He doesn't miss," Manolo says.

The Operator looks down at his feet to avoid Bacas's gaze. "Did you know it would be a suicide mission?" he says to his shoes.

"I had a feeling there would be a lot of security. But it wasn't a suicide mission, was it? You all made it back alive!" Bacas says.

"Yes, we did, but without him we wouldn't have made it. You didn't know how good he was when you sent us," Manolo says.

"Well, I had faith in you and Ludavico. Don't forget that."

Manolo shuffles his feet. "Another thing. The Enforcer we killed . . . it was . . . you."

"How could it be me? I'm right here!"

"Well, he was asleep, just like Greyson said he would be.

But when he turned over, it was you. You had shaved but there was no mistaking it. We all stood there and the stranger took it upon himself to shoot him in the heart."

"Is that so?" Bacas says, with a look at the Operator.

The Operator looks up and meets Bacas's blue gaze. "They hesitated, yes, but it was definitely your face."

Are all chief Enforcers androids? Do they all share the same face? If so, would the others get upset when they found out one of the lower-level Enforcers killed one from a higher level? Greyson made it seem like the government ordered the hit, but could Bacas have gone rogue?

"So, you thought it was me and you took the shot anyways?" Bacas says.

"Just following orders. It isn't my place to ask questions," the Operator says.

Bacas stares at the Operator for a tense moment before he breaks into a wide smile. "I like this guy," he says to Manolo. "He has what it takes. From the sound of it, I should have sent him alone. He is worth five of you rats."

Manolo hangs his head in shame. The Operator is about to open his mouth to come to the defense of the other men before he thinks better of it and stays silent.

"That's enough for one day. Go rest your souls. If I need you I will send for you," Bacas says.

Outside of Suerte the Operator grabs Manolo by the sleeve and turns the man so they are face to face. "You shouldn't have told Bacas everything like that. You could've made it seem like we had worked together to escape instead of giving me all the credit."

"We owe you our lives. Besides, Bacas should know about your skills with a blaster so he can put them to good use against the Sisters."

"What is it with you and the Sisters? The way I see it, if you could learn to work together it could be a very powerful partnership. Beneficial for all of Gamma."

"We don't want to work with them, we want to get their recipe and take over their production. Greyson has tried to get Bacas to see the benefits of controlling the distribution of Serum but Bacas won't listen. With you by our side we could do it ourselves."

"You would go against Bacas?"

"He hasn't explicitly stated that he doesn't want to take over production; he just won't authorize the attack. It would be a gift."

"I'll tell you right now Bacas wouldn't like it. Members of his district killed by his own men? I want no part of it."

Manolo looks at the Operator in disgust. "Greyson was right, you are a sympathizer. You work for them, don't you?"

"No, I don't. I'm just speaking from an outsider's perspective," the Operator says.

Manolo looks at him with suspicion dripping from his pores. "I need to talk to Greyson," he says. He rips his arm away from the Operator's grasp and leaves the Operator alone in front of Suerte.

27

THE TROUBLE

Fᴇɴɪx sᴛᴀɴᴅs up when the Operator walks into the pool hall. Miguel sits at the bar, next to the two androids, with Fenix on the ground by his feet. The dog barks twice before his nose tells him his friend has returned. Miguel turns around, ready to greet a potential patron with a cheesy smile, and sees the Operator. The smile lines around his eyes transform to those of recognition and he turns back around to his drink.

The Operator bends over and scratches Fenix behind the ears. He walks to the side of the bar with the dog on his heels. He pauses and looks at Miguel before he goes behind the bar.

"Do you mind?" he says, and points to the glasses under the mirror.

"Help yourself."

The Operator takes a glass and pours himself a glass of Serum from the bottle under the counter.

"You were gone early," Miguel says.

"Bacas wanted us to go to Sigma and take care of an Enforcer on the tenth," the Operator says. He walks back around the bar and sits on the barstool next to Miguel. Fenix circles three times before he lies down between the two men.

"That's where these two come from," Miguel says.

"I know. I dealt with a lot of their kind today," the Operator says. He sinks into the chair, his legs grateful for the rest.

"Get into a bit of trouble over there?"

"Just a bit. I'm starving. Have you eaten yet?" he asks the pool hall owner.

"Not since breakfast, amigo, what about you?"

"Same for me."

"I think there is some food left from earlier, feel free to help yourself," Miguel says.

"What do you say we go to the intersection and get some food? Do you have a favorite spot?"

"My friend owns one of the carts. Best soup in the city. There is a spicy broth with some meat and potatoes, it's amazing."

"What kind of meat is it?"

"Beats me. To be honest I don't want to know."

The two men leave the pool hall and Fenix follows behind. A light drizzle falls, and the two men walk close to the building.

"Have him walk with us next to the building," Miguel says, with a nod to Fenix. "The rain will burn his skin if he gets too wet."

"Burn him?"

"Yes, it's acidic. Happens when the reclaimers need to be emptied. The toxins the reclaimers are designed to pull out gather and then it rains below the third. The rats know to hide."

The Operator looks around and realizes the streets arc empty of rats. "Come here, Fenix," the Operator says. He follows the command with a whistle. Fenix comes over to walk with the Operator next to the building. Beads of water sit on the dog's fur. The Operator reaches down and brushes the water off his friend, then wipes his hand on his jacket.

"How long does it take to burn? Will I know right away?" the Operator asks.

"It'll take more than that. You have to be exposed for a while, in rain stronger than this. Fenix would have probably been all right, but it's better to be safe than sorry."

The dog stays close to the two men on their way to the intersection.

Everyone in the intersection takes care to stay away from the streams of water that drip from the edges of the canopy overhead. Three separate times, the Operator sees what he thinks could be one of the twins but, each time he looks closer, he finds a random person. He thinks about how dense the people are packed in beneath the canopy and wonders if, to someone on the upper levels, this many people would look like the fluid flow of rats he watched struggle to get into the trash can. He is surprised there aren't more rats that take shelter under the canopy, but with so many people here, there wouldn't be much room for them.

Miguel's friend owns a cart in the center. There is just enough room for someone to walk between his cart and the two on either side of his. These three carts are the only ones in the center; the rest are in a ring around the edges. The two men and the dog stand in the crowd of people in front of the three carts and wait to move forward.

The smell of food overpowers the smell of wet, unwashed people as the men get closer to the cart. The owner of the cart spots Miguel and waves him forward. The other customers glare at the two men as they make their way through the crowd to where soup is ladled out in plastic bowls.

"Miguel! It's been forever, amigo," the cart owner says. He reaches out his hand and the two men clasp each other's forearms.

"I know, I don't get out much," Miguel says. He turns to the

Operator. "This is Benny. Best soup in the district. No, the city!"

"You don't need to flatter me, Miguel, you know you already get the discount," Benny says with a wink. "Getting the usual today?"

"Sure am. I'll need two," Miguel says, holding up two fingers.

"You got it," the cart owner says.

Miguel slaps the Operator on the back. "Trust me, you'll like it," he says.

Benny ladles soup into two bowls. "Be careful, it's hot. Stand away from the crowd, people have no respect around here. They'll push you aside to get where they're going."

The Operator raises a finger to edge himself into the conversation. "Do you have any biscuits? Or anything a dog could eat?"

Benny leans over the front of his cart and looks down at Fenix. The dog wags his tail. "Sure do," Benny says. He reaches into a container. "Here you go," he says as he drops a biscuit down to the dog.

Miguel and the Operator are careful to balance their bowls as they walk to the edge of the canopy. They stand with their backs to the open air and keep an eye on the people who walk in front of them in case they get too close. The broth is spicy—not the type of spicy that burns the mouth, but the type that warms the insides. The meat is chewy—not enough to be unpleasant, but enough to make the Operator wonder how long ago the creature had been killed. He has a vague suspicion that he has found out where some of the rats have gone.

The Operator finishes his soup and turns to look at the empty street behind him. The haze has gotten darker and the Operator wonders if he would see the sunset if he were still in the badlands.

When Miguel finishes his soup, the two men walk back to the pool hall. On another night, one where he is not so tired, he might stay out and see what entertainment the intersection has to offer. The Operator makes sure that Fenix stays out of the rain and wonders if the dog misses the simplicity of the badlands as much as he does.

———

MIGUEL IS surprised to see the door of the pool hall open even though it's never locked. He rushes ahead to check on his establishment, with Fenix close on his heels. The march between districts with Ludavico on his back has worn the Operator down and his legs refuse to pick up speed. He can't remember the last time he felt so exhausted.

How long did it take for Ludavico to get medical attention? Is he okay? Does Ludavico share Manolo's conviction about what their group should do to the Sisters? How many other men has Greyson been able to convince?

The Operator walks in after Miguel has completed his inspection. From what both men can tell, nothing seems to have been touched.

"Damn, must've just missed them!" Miguel says.

Did Miguel think he missed a potential customer or did he want to catch a burglar in the act? Was this supposed to be a message for the Operator, that anybody who wants to get to him only has to walk through an unlocked door? Is the message from the White Jackets or from someone under Greyson's thumb? Maybe the two androids at the bar scared off whoever opened the door. Maybe they are good for something after all.

"What'd you think of the soup?" Miguel says.

"It was good. Perfect food for the rain."

"Agreed. Want anything to drink before we call it a night?" Miguel says from behind the bar.

"No thanks, I'm going to head to bed," the Operator says. He taps his leg twice and Fenix follows him to the storage room.

"Sleep well," Miguel says. He has his hands on his hips and continues to look around the room for something, anything, out of place.

The Operator doesn't bother to take his clothes off before he lies down. He falls asleep with Fenix next to him, the same way they did when they were in the badlands and had to sleep next to each other for warmth.

Hands around the Operator's throat wake him up. Thumbs dig into his windpipe. His own hands shoot up to pry himself free. The room is dark and he can't see his attacker. Shadows above him are fuzzy as his vision blurs from the lack of oxygen. His blaster is at his side, never more than an arm's reach away. His right arm reaches out, grabs the weapon, and begins to bring it to where his attacker's head should be when he feels another pair of hands rip the blaster from his grasp.

His left hand claws at the face over him and he lifts his legs into the air. His plan is to wrap his legs around the attacker's head in order to pry the man away from his throat. The attacker leans forward and is able to keep his head away from the Operator's searching feet. The Operator uses his knees to batter his assailant. He pummels the man on top of him in the back. The hands around his neck loosen with each blow.

There isn't much time left. His vision fades fast and, in a moment, he won't even be able to make out the two shadows. He calls upon his last bits of oxygen and uses both hands to push the attacker's face away from his own. There is a struggle to keep the man's head down but, with a final push, the Operator is able to hook a foot under his chin. He extends his leg and the attacker falls in front of him.

The Operator leans to his right and takes two ragged breaths. Whoever pulled the blaster away takes the opportunity to stand up, and the Operator sees their shadow take aim. The Operator lunges just as the trigger is pulled, and the shadow's legs are taken out. Glass shatters and is followed by the sound of liquid pouring onto the floor. The man falls backwards and the blaster slides across the floor. The Operator searches for his attacker's face with his hands before he feels a forearm wrap around his neck. He is lifted up and back and comes to rest with his back on the other attacker's chest, his throat squeezed with increasing force.

The attacker who missed his shot grabs the Operator's legs, immobilizing him. His hands struggle against the arm to give him space to breathe, but the arm around his neck is buried deep in his windpipe. His senses fade out one by one. His hearing is the last to go. Fenix barks but it sounds like it comes from deep within a well. The well gets deeper as the rest of his oxygen runs out and everything fades to black.

28

THE SAVIOR

THE OPERATOR IS SHAKEN AWAKE. He doubles over and coughs, his throat on fire. He tries to sit up and is forced onto his back by hands on each of his shoulders. His eyes ache from the pressure in his skull but he is able to make out enough of Miguel's face in front of his own to know the struggle for his life is over. Fenix jumps onto the Operator's chest and licks his face.

"What happened?" the Operator croaks. He takes long, steady breaths and focuses on each exhale, a new appreciation for this automatic task. He tries to lift his head, to see the room around him, but the pain in his eyes makes him change his mind, so he lies back down.

"The androids. They woke up," Miguel says. "I took Fenix outside for his morning walk and we weren't even halfway to his favorite spot before he started whining. He kept trying to go back. I tried to urge him forward but he wouldn't listen. Eventually I gave up and followed him back. He would run forward, wait for me to catch up, and run forward again."

The Operator's hand finds Fenix's head and begins to pet the dog while Miguel tells him what happened.

"Fenix rushed all the way to your door. When I got in here

the androids were on top of you! Your blaster was on the floor inside the door. I bent over to pick it up and I wrestled with one of them before I was able to shoot him right in the stomach. Fenix bit the face of the android choking you but the guy didn't budge."

Miguel leans forward and runs his hand down the length of the dog's spine before he pats him twice on the rump. "The android looked at me with those dead eyes of his and I shot him right in the face, point-blank. I finished the other one off with a shot to the back of his head."

"You said they were from Sigma, right?" the Operator asks.

Miguel grabs the face of one of the limp androids and opens their lips to inspect the pointed teeth. "That's right. You were in Sigma yesterday, weren't you? Think they were ordered to kill you? I didn't think a signal could travel so far through the interference from the haze."

"Neither did I, but I guess they were still able to receive orders. I wonder if someone planted them here in case of emergency," the Operator says.

"Killing you doesn't seem like an emergency. Do you think there are other androids planted throughout Gamma? Not just from Sigma but from Theta too? Maybe Gamma has androids planted in the other districts as well . . ."

"There's no way to tell. Who would keep track? We both know there isn't any central authority down here. Above the reclaimers the government uses sensors to track every android that moves between the different levels, not between districts. To be honest I doubt anyone up there even remembers where the district lines lie."

"You don't think Bacas wants to know when another district's android crosses into Gamma?"

"Any androids this far down would be outdated: easy to identify and and easier to hack. I guess he doesn't bother to track them because there aren't usually androids this far down. Plus, they would be seized by anyone who found them before he could collect them."

"Their dead eyes give them away," says Miguel.

"In these models, yes. In the upper levels, past the twenty-fifth, androids are harder to distinguish from humans. You would need to have a full conversation with one to realize they are different. Beyond the fiftieth, it's almost impossible. There are signs, but unless you are trained for the task there is no way to know whether or not someone is human. That's why the government is so strict about tracking each and every one of them," the Operator says. The memory of him and Patrice on vacation raises goosebumps on every inch of his skin. What would the government have done if they found out he was with an android who jumped between levels untracked? Could he be thrown in jail?

"Wait, how do you know so much about the levels above the fiftieth?" Miguel says with a mixture of suspicion and awe.

"I was born there."

"Are you serious? What are you doing down here? I have never heard of anyone down so many levels from where they were born," Miguel says. "How many have you fallen?"

"Well, I was born on the fifty-second. But I've been as high as the seventy-fourth."

Miguel's eyes widen. The upper levels seem like another planet to him and now the Operator seems like an alien, someone born into a situation very different from his own. "Were you banished? What did you do?"

"I wasn't banished, I left. The upper levels aren't what you think they are. Everyone and everything hides their true nature behind a polished exterior."

Miguel stands still as he takes in what the Operator has just told him. It must be difficult to hear for someone who was born on the surface, someone who has only ever dreamed of what life on the upper levels must be like.

"So, you left the city," Miguel says.

"Yes, I needed to get away from it all. It was only recently that I thought I was strong enough to come back to the city and avoid the temptation of the upper levels." The temptation of Patrice pulls at the Operator from up high. He closes his eyes to hold a tear between his eyelids and pets Fenix to avoid thoughts of her.

"What did you do outside the city with all that time?" Miguel asks, unable to wrap his head around this new information about the Operator. "The badlands are a lot different from the upper levels. It must have been quite a shock."

"Not as different as you'd think. There are still things out to get you and you have to be careful all the time." The Operator opens his eyes, stares at the ceiling for a moment, then looks at the pool hall owner. "To be honest with you, I got good at being alone until Fenix showed up."

The Operator begins to prop himself onto his elbow, but Miguel puts his hand on his chest and forces the man back down onto the bed.

"You need to rest," Miguel says.

The Operator grabs Miguel's hand and removes it from his chest. Firmer than he had intended, but the point is made.

"I need to go to Suerte," the Operator says as he sits up. Fenix looks at the Operator as if he understands the words of his companion and would reproach him if he was able to speak.

Vials of Stim litter the ground, the contents of the boxes that had surrounded the Operator before the struggle with the androids.

"Why is there Stim in here, Miguel?" the Operator asks.

Miguel hangs his head. "Bacas pays me to store his surplus. Nobody else knows about it, not even Greyson."

"And now me. So you've been working for Bacas this whole time?"

"Most everybody works for Bacas in some shape or form. There are stores of Stim all over the district."

"So that's how you make your money . . ." the Operator says, his words trailing away.

"Nobody comes to the pool hall. I had to do something. He didn't really give me a choice in the matter."

"And you didn't think to mention this before?"

"What does it matter? If I didn't keep the boxes here he would arrest me and keep them here anyways. I leave the door unlocked hoping someone will come in here and steal it all."

The Operator watches Miguel collect the vials from the ground and wonders how much it's all worth. "He's made all of Gamma complicit in his plans to rob the government."

"There's nothing we can do. He arrests anyone who doesn't listen," says Miguel.

The Operator hears Iris's words: *Cut off the head and the body dies.* "There's something I can do," the Operator says as he begins to stand up.

Miguel puts his hand on the Operator's shoulder and forces him back down. "You can't do anything if you don't take care of your body. Rest! It's still early. I'll wake you up in an hour. Then you can go to Suerte."

Fenix's eyes show his concern and the Operator knows the pool hall owner is right.

"Fine. One hour." He lays his head back down. Fenix lies beside him and Miguel leaves the two of them alone, shutting the door behind him. Sleep wraps her arm around the Operator's neck and doesn't let go.

29

THE THREAT

The Operator doesn't get to Suerte until lunchtime after Miguel lets him sleep the morning away. Ludavico sits with other gang members at the middle round table in the back of the room. The blond man's head is wrapped in gauze and his eyes have the glazed look of someone pumped full of Serum. Every spoonful of soup raised to his lips is slurped with care. The rest of the men at the table tear into meat that sits on a tray in the middle of the table. Everyone at the table stops their meal when they notice the Operator approach.

"He's here today thanks to you!" one of the twins yells out with a nod to his bandaged comrade.

The men at the table all hold up their glasses. "Cheers," the second twin cries out. "To the stranger!"

"To the stranger!" the men all say in unison.

"Come on over here," Bacas says from his corner. He waves the person next to him out of their seat and gestures for the Operator to sit down. He beckons to the bartender as the man of the hour takes a seat.

"The twins told me the same story about yesterday," Bacas says before he takes a sip of Serum. "About how many androids you eliminated." He sets his glass on the table. The men around Ludavico pretend to eat their lunch but, from the volume of their silence, the Operator assumes they hang onto every word.

"They said something I found upsetting though," Bacas says. He rolls his glass on its base and the liquid inside swirls.

The men at the other table all freeze, some of them midbite.

"Really? What is that?" the Operator says. He tries to sound nonchalant.

"Well, they said you might be a better shot than me!" Bacas throws his head back and laughs. The men at the other table all chuckle as if they know something the Operator doesn't.

Bacas continues, "You were stimmed, so that has to be taken into account. But the twins swear up and down that if we were both stimmed it would be hard to tell who's better."

"Hmm," the Operator says to buy some time while he organizes his thoughts. "Funny you say that. I was trying to save my own skin too, not just his. Self-preservation brings out the best in me." A plate of food is brought out and placed on the table in front of him. Brown meat, source unknown, and a boiled potato, all of it covered in thick brown gravy with mysterious lumps. The Operator slices off a piece of potato, now aware he didn't eat before he left the pool hall. Bland but hot, the gravy salty, the most he could have expected.

"Maybe we should have a contest to see who really is the best," Bacas says. He pulls out his blaster, the one with coils around the barrel, and weighs the weapon in his hand. He looks around the casino to find a target.

"I'll concede defeat. I wouldn't be able to shoot well now anyways, I have a bit of a headache," the Operator says.

The men at the other table chuckle.

"Scared to lose?" Greyson says from behind the Operator. He walks around the table, tells the man on the other side of Bacas to get lost, and sits down.

"Not scared, just trying to enjoy my lunch. Maybe some other time," the Operator says. He tries to cut the meat with his fork but, when he finds it too tough to cut without a knife, he stabs the meat and tears a piece off with his teeth. Chewy and not even close to as flavorful as the meat in Benny's soup last night. No wonder they smothered it with gravy.

"Should we stim first?" Bacas says. He pulls two fresh vials from his pocket.

"Well, I already have my own," the Operator says. He pulls the two unused vials from his pocket.

"Where did you get those?" Greyson demands to know. The Operator ignores him and looks at Bacas. From the look on the chief Enforcer's face he can tell the man has no questions about where these two vials came from.

"You stole them!" Greyson yells when the Operator ignores his question. He slams his fist on the table. "Bacas, let me take him out back and shoot him. We don't need a thief around here!"

"You don't know what you are talking about," the Operator says, as if he is a patient schoolteacher waiting for his pupil to understand the lesson.

"Bacas! Let's make an example of him," Greyson pleads.

"You heard the man. Now shut up," Bacas says to Greyson.

Greyson sits with a blank stare on his face, unable to comprehend.

"Those are the Stims we gave you yesterday, aren't they?" Bacas says to the Operator. The Serum in his glass is swirled again.

"They are," the Operator says. He takes another bite of potato.

"You did all of that without Stim?" Ludavico says from the next table. The whole table of men turn to look in awe at the Operator.

Bacas stands up. "Leave," he says to the group of men at the next table. "Now!" he yells. The men all leave their food on the table and grumble as they make their way out of the casino.

"You too," Bacas says to Greyson when he sees that the man by his side hasn't moved. With a violent push against the table, Greyson stands up and follows the rest of the gang.

"Where did you learn to shoot like that?" Bacas says to the Operator when the two of them are alone. "An upper-level guy like you has no business handling a blaster like that."

The fact that Bacas knows he is from the upper levels isn't lost on the Operator. "I spent a lot of time in the badlands with nothing to do but practice."

"So that's where you went when you left," Bacas says as he sits back down.

The Operator can't tell if this is a statement or a question. "How did you find out?" he says.

"The search we did the other day," Bacas says. "The woman you asked me to look up only has one brother and he currently works for the government on the sixty-first. I thought to myself, 'Why would this guy be so interested in this woman?' There must be some way you know her. I did some digging and found footage of the two of you on vacation. You were much softer then but there is no mistaking it's you."

The Operator leans back in his chair, his appetite gone, waiting for Bacas to continue.

"I dug some more and things got strange. She has a government file, which makes sense, but no birth certificate. I looked up her parents and found out her dad is a developer with the android security agency."

Bacas mirrors the Operator and leans back himself. "Can you tell me why she exists without being born?"

The Operator stares at Bacas. He doesn't utter a word and tries to keep his expression blank.

"Don't worry, I'll tell you," Bacas says. He takes a drink of Serum. "It's because she is an android. But you knew that, didn't you?"

Bacas studies the Operator's face to see his reaction and finds none.

"Now, I am going to need something from you. It's not too complicated. Simple, really. I need you to walk across the rails and kill the Sisters."

The Operator breaks his silence. "They haven't done anything. I won't do it."

"You will. If you don't, then I'll have to take Patrice's life from her. Not literally—she isn't technically alive. No, I will expose her secret to the world and make sure everyone knows she is an android. Including her. It's fascinating, I don't think she even knows what she is."

Bacas walks over to the bar, grabs his computer, and sits back down. "I've never heard of an android who experiences emotions before. She may be one of the first. Watch this." He types into the computer and turns the screen around to show the Operator a video.

The video is from the surveillance camera in an elevator. It shows Patrice from above as she walks inside and selects her destination. As soon as the doors close her back hits the wall behind her and she falls to the ground, her hands over her face. Her chest heaves with every sob.

The Operator can feel his eyes get wet but he is able to keep the tears from falling.

"This video was taken just after she found out she can't have children. From what I can tell, the doctors never told her she is an android. If her father is that good they might not have known either."

Bacas plays the video on a loop. She enters the elevator again, falls to the ground again, sobs again.

"Imagine how she will feel if I expose her secret to the world. A secret she doesn't even know herself," Bacas says.

She enters the elevator a third time.

"She will be devastated," the Operator manages to say. The words choke out and he is sure that Bacas is able to detect the emotion in his voice. He tries to think of her as an android, tries to recall his own embarrassment when he found out, tries to convince himself that maybe, just maybe, she deserves it. The fact she doesn't know she's an android provides the answer to the question that has nagged him from the day he found out her secret. She was also a pawn in her father's game and didn't trick him on purpose.

"I'll do it," the Operator whispers.

"Good," says Bacas. He turns the computer back around to face himself and slams it shut. "Tonight. I will give you all the Stim you need but I have a feeling you won't use it."

"Tonight?"

"Unless you want her secret to get out," Bacas says. "It's your call."

"I'll do it tonight," the Operator says, defeated.

30

THE GAUNTLET

MIGUEL TRIES in vain to get the Operator to reconsider from the other side of the bar. "Bacas is crazy! Who cares if he tells everyone she is an android. They probably won't even believe him!"

"I care," the Operator says.

"Isn't she the reason you went to the badlands in the first place?"

"Yes," the Operator says, dejected. He hasn't touched the glass of Serum Miguel set down in front of him over five minutes ago. His eyes, unfocused, stare at the space between himself and the drink.

"Are you going to take Fenix with you?" Miguel says.

"This could be my last adventure. I think he would want to take part."

"No way you can shoot your way through, too many White Jackets are willing to die for them."

"I might not have to shoot my way in. I have been over to talk to them before so I should be able to get an audience without too much trouble. I could kill them then."

"But you could never leave. The White Jackets would make sure of that."

"I know. That's why I've *considered* shooting my way in. If I decide to, I could make it through most if not all of the White Jackets. I wouldn't have to worry about them on the way out. Might not make it to the Sisters though."

"Sounds like both options end with you dead. Which do you think has the best chance of survival?"

"Not sure. That's part of the reason I want Fenix to come with me, I need to see his reaction to the situation. When he barks I'll know it's time for me to act. If that happens at the sight of the first White Jackets then I will shoot my way through them. If he waits until we are with the Sisters I will shoot my way out."

"What if he doesn't bark at all?"

"I can cross that bridge when I get there."

"You're going to let a dog decide your fate?" Miguel says, astonished.

"Not just any dog. My dog." The Operator pushes the glass of Serum back across the bar towards Miguel.

"When will you go? Middle of the night?"

"No, I don't want to wait that long. Think they're eating dinner right now?" the Operator asks.

"Most people are," Miguel says.

"I suppose now is as good a time as any," the Operator says.

He stands up and pats his leg twice. Fenix gets up from the ground and stands at the Operator's side.

"Are you sure about this, amigo?"

"I have to do this, Miguel." He reaches his arm out to the pool hall owner and the two men clasp each other's forearms.

"I'll see you again, in this life or the next," the Operator says.

"Let's make it this one. Good luck," says Miguel.

Night has fallen on the surface. With Fenix at his side it

feels like another one of their adventures in the badlands, except out there they could see for miles, and in the city it is hard to see more than ten feet through the haze. Manolo and Ludavico are with Greyson in the bazaar. The Operator avoids eye contact with Greyson and nods at the other two men. The two men pretend not to see him. He doesn't have to turn around to know the three men follow him to the station.

Fenix walks a few feet in front of him. He seems to understand where they are headed but there is no way he knows the reason why.

Thoughts of Patrice drift into the Operator's mind. She lives on the eighty-first and can't have kids. Does she remember him or did her father wipe that memory from her mind? He thinks about how nice it would be to be an android so he could have painful memories erased. A much easier way to deal with his addiction. If he could have her erased, Bacas wouldn't be able to send him on a suicide mission. Does Bacas keep every memory, or does he extract them when they are no longer needed?

The bloodstains on the rails remind the Operator of the murdered White Jackets. It seems like so long ago. Whatever happened to the government blaster in the tunnels that belonged to Greyson? Will Klepsydra be upset when he shows up without the evidence he promised to bring? Assuming he doesn't shoot his way in. If he does, the tattooed Sister will be upset for a different reason.

On the Sister's side of the midline the Operator half expects the White Jackets to shoot him on sight. His eyes search for the potential ambush in case they got wind of the real reason he has come across. Fenix walks towards the broken bridge without a care in the world, unaware they are in enemy territory. The Operator follows his dog's lead and tries to appear to be just as carefree.

The street that runs parallel to the rails is deserted. It's like the city itself waits to spring the trap and every appendage stays still so their plan isn't uncovered. Not even the random rat is out to deliver a message. Fenix continues at his relaxed pace. A light rain begins to fall. The Operator calls out to Fenix and makes sure the two of them walk next to the buildings in order to take advantage of whatever shelter the city can provide.

Three White Jackets huddle under an awning in the intersection up ahead. The broken bridge is behind them and they face the strip of neon signs that runs perpendicular to the rails. The floodlight behind them casts long shadows to the opposite side of the street, where the Operator and Fenix walk. The shadows grope at the feet of the Operator and his dog as the foreigners turn right and begin to walk beneath faded neon signs.

Fenix loses confidence about their ultimate destination and begins to walk behind the Operator. The sign for the tavern shines through the haze. Two more White Jackets stand guard outside the large metal door. Stim is limited on this side of the midline, so the two White Jackets who stand guard can't be stimmed if they are able to stand still. If they were to motion towards their weapons, the Operator knows he will be able to draw faster and eliminate the threat, provided Fenix gives the signal.

"That's where we are headed," the Operator tells Fenix. He looks down and finds the dog has slowed down and is now more than five feet behind him. "Come on, boy, there's nothing to worry about." The Operator wonders if the dog can detect the lie. Fenix jogs forward and walks right next to the Operator.

If he were to turn around he would still see the three White Jackets beneath the awning in the intersection. What he wouldn't see is the dozens of blasters aimed at his head from the windows on the second level.

31

THE DISCUSSION

"I need to see the Sisters," the Operator says to the two guards outside the door to the tavern.

"Piss off," the guard on the left side of the door says. They spit on the ground in front of the Operator's feet.

"I need to see the Sisters," he says again.

The guard on the right side of the door draws his blaster from its holster. The Operator stares down the barrel of the gun at the blue eyes behind the sights.

"You heard her! Piss off. Nobody gets in without getting past us."

That would be easy to arrange. The Operator looks at Fenix. Even one bark would be enough for the Operator to know to shoot his way through, but the dog sits still and stares past the two guards to the door behind them.

"He can't help you," one of the guards says with a laugh.

The Operator follows Fenix's lead and stands still, stares at the door. He flexes his jaw.

"Do you want to hit me?" the White Jacket on the left says. She sticks her chin out. "Go ahead, I'll give you the first shot."

The door opens and Iris rushes forward, grabs the blaster

still in the Operator's face, and forces it to aim at the ground. "Let him in. Can't you see he is alone? What can one man do?" she says.

One man and his dog.

Both guards' eyes narrow with suspicion. "Stay here and guard the door," Iris says. She turns around and walks into the tavern. Fenix trots in behind her. The Operator brings up the rear.

The Operator counts six White Jackets in the smoky tavern. He is sure there are more ready to come inside if they are needed. Iris leads them to the poker table in the back of the smoky tavern. "Sit," she says as she pulls a chair out. Fenix lies down on the ground without hesitation and the Operator, following his dog's lead, sits down. Iris takes a seat across from the Operator.

The Operator wastes no time. "I was sent here by Bacas to kill you and Klepsydra," he says. The words hang in the air a moment before Iris is able to inhale them.

"Alone?" she says.

"I have Fenix," he says. He reaches down and scratches the dog behind the ears.

"And how do you expect to complete your mission? If you shoot me, they"—she looks at the men behind the Operator—"would kill you before you were able to make it out the front door."

Unless some of them were able to stim before the shooting began, the Operator doesn't think six White Jackets would stand a chance. He hopes the situation doesn't come to that.

The Sister watches the Operator weigh his options. "It isn't smart. Klepsydra isn't even here. If you were to kill me you would still have to go find her."

"I have a feeling that, if I were to kill you, she would find me," the Operator says.

The door behind the table opens and Klepsydra walks into the tavern. The Operator looks at Iris and raises an eyebrow. "You were saying?"

"Did you bring the boy?" Klepsydra says. She isn't one to waste time either.

"He didn't. He says he is here to kill us," Iris says to her Sister. "Bacas's order."

The Operator nods in agreement.

Both Sisters stare at the Operator, unsure of what to do in the situation.

"Come work for us," Iris says. "You can help us take him down. The government needs to know how he conducts his business."

The Operator thinks about Patrice. "I can't do that," the Operator says with finality.

"Why not?" Klepsydra says.

"You wouldn't understand."

Fenix lifts his head and the Operator thinks it might be time to draw his weapon. The dog lays his head back down on his front paws. At this rate, who knows when the shoot-out will begin.

"So what should we do?" Klepsydra says. "You didn't bring the witness. We told you what would happen if you came on our side without reason. We might as well kill you now and get it over with."

"There is still something I can provide even if I don't work for you," the Operator says. "Evidence against Greyson."

"You were supposed to bring the evidence with you already! We will get the midliner ourselves," Klepsydra says.

"Does the boy even exist?" Iris asks. Her tender voice doesn't align with the situation.

"He does, his name is Usryd. The others wouldn't take me to him last time but—"

"You said you would bring him to us!" Klepsydra says. She slams her hands on the table.

"It's not that simple," the Operator says. He stares at the tattooed Sister, his hand ready to grab his blaster at a sign from Fenix.

"You went into the tunnels?" Iris says. Her hand moves to lie over her sister's right hand. "Tell us what you know."

"Usryd grabbed Greyson's blaster after the murder. He is scared of the thing, afraid it would make him want to kill. He had to take time away from the rest of his group."

"Why should we care?" Klepsydra says.

"Government blasters record every shot fired."

"Lies!" Klepsydra explodes. "More lies! There is no blaster! You are trying to save yourself again! I should have killed you in the pool hall." She rips her hand from beneath her sister's and draws her weapon from her side. She points it down at the Operator in his seat.

The Operator checks on Fenix from the corner of his eye. The dog doesn't move.

"Sit down," Iris tells Klepsydra. She turns to the Operator. "And why couldn't you grab it and bring it to us?"

"Usryd took it with him when he left. I need to go back to the midline but didn't have the chance before Bacas sent me to kill the two of you. And here we are." The Operator looks at Klepsydra. "To be fair, I still have a few more days to get the midliner to you, according to our original agreement."

"With the memory from the boy and the blaster, Greyson would be finished," Iris says out loud to nobody in particular.

Fenix picks his head up and looks around at the tavern. Is he about to bark? He gets up and walks to the front door as if he forgot something outside. The Operator understands it is time to go.

"Exactly," the Operator says. "I need to go back. Shoot me

in the back if you wish." He gets up from the table and follows his dog to the exit.

"What will happen when Bacas finds out you didn't kill us?" Klepsydra calls out.

"Not sure," the Operator says as he marches through the White Jackets on the way out. They all stare at him and wait for the order to shoot.

"You still owe us the evidence against Greyson," Iris says.

"I need more time," says the Operator. The Sisters talk between themselves behind him as he opens the door.

"There is no blaster!" Klepsydra says.

"Let's give him the time he needs."

"Let's kill him and be done with it!"

"No harm can come from letting him live. Bacas might even kill him and remove the problem from our plates."

"And if he doesn't?"

"Trust me, Sister," says Iris.

The door to the tavern shuts behind the Operator and all he can hear is the sound of his heart in the silence of the street.

32

THE PRISONER

The Operator pauses on the bottom step when he sees movement on the opposite platform. Three men sit on the bottom steps across the station. The Operator can't see their faces but one of them has blond hair. Ludavico. The other two must be Greyson and Manolo. Fenix is a few steps ahead so, in order to get the dog to come back to his side, the Operator taps his leg twice. Fenix looks at the Operator and tilts his head sideways instead of rushing back to his human.

"Come here," the Operator whispers. He holds his thumb and forefinger close to the ground as if he has a treat. The dog doesn't move.

The Operator looks down the darkness of the tunnel on his left where he chased the two midliners. If he could somehow make it down the length of the platform and get into the tunnel, he could find Usryd and the blaster, sneak back up to the Sisters, and deliver them their evidence. They might even be able to convince the government that Bacas knew about the murders and did nothing to enforce the law in his jurisdiction. Greyson would probably say he acted alone, serve his punishment, and rejoin Bacas later in time with increased prestige for his time in prison.

The only question is how to get to the tunnel? He could try and sneak along the wall on his side of the station. There is a good chance the men won't see him but, if they do, he would make an easy target. Could he make a break for it? They would see him streak down the platform and would give chase. There is only so far he could make it in the tunnels with the three men behind him. Also, his back would be exposed, a position he'd rather avoid.

And what about Fenix? If the dog doesn't make the leap from the platform he will have to grab him before he can run into the tunnel. Without the dog's nose he would get lost in the tunnels. Maybe he could scoop Fenix up, carry him while he runs, then let him go after the jump.

While the Operator has his eyes on the tunnel and tries to decide which plan would work best he doesn't pay attention to Fenix. The dog has walked to the edge of the platform, and the Operator looks over in time to see Fenix disappear onto the rails below. The men across the station see the movement of the dog on the rails and stand up to investigate. As they get closer to the rails the Operator can see that along with Ludavico and Greyson is one of the twins, not Manolo.

"Shit," the Operator says to himself. He followed the dog's lead with the Sisters and it worked out; he might as well follow the dog now. When will he have the chance to go into the tunnels and get the blaster from the midliner?

Greyson calls out to the Operator from across the rails. "That was quick," he says.

Fenix walks across the rails, calm as can be, and looks back at the Operator when he gets to the far platform. The Operator, when he catches up, reaches down and helps his friend onto the platform before he pulls himself up.

"You didn't do it, did you?" Greyson says when they are face to face.

"No, I didn't," the Operator says.

Greyson pulls out his blaster and aims it at the Operator's head. "Do you know what happens when someone disobeys a direct order?" he asks.

"No, I don't," the Operator says. Too many blasters have been in his face today.

"You are about to find out."

The three men take the Operator back to Suerte. Fenix follows behind like this is another one of their strolls through the streets. The Operator wishes the dog would bark so he could start shooting. Sometimes it's hard to trust the instincts of others when they can't vocalize the rationale behind their thoughts.

Once inside Suerte, Greyson uses the end of his blaster to shove the Operator into the open seat in front of Bacas. "Sit," he says.

Bacas looks at the Operator's jacket, which is covered with the same dust, without a drop of blood in sight. "Is it done?" Bacas says.

"No," the Operator tells him, defiant.

Bacas stays calm when given the news, as if he expected this result. He leans forward and folds his hands on the table. "And why not? You know what this means, don't you? For them? You had the chance to kill them quickly. I prefer to take my time."

The Operator looks down at Fenix lying next to his chair and says nothing.

"Well? Why didn't you kill them?" Bacas says, eyebrows raised.

"You won't believe me if I told you."

"Try me."

"He didn't let me know the time was right for them to die," the Operator says, gesturing with his lips to Fenix.

"The dog!" Greyson exclaims. "You disobeyed a direct order from a chief Enforcer because of your *dog*?"

Fenix must be able to tell the two men are talking about him because he stands up with his eyes on Bacas. His tail drops and he crouches down. A low growl emanates from his throat.

The Operator knows what this means: it's time for him to pull out his blaster and shoot his way out of the casino. Thoughts of Patrice bubble to the surface and he hesitates. If he kills Bacas, will her secret be safe? Did he tell anyone else about her?

This moment of hesitation gives Bacas time to stand up, draw his blaster, and shoot Fenix in the head. The dog's life spills on the floor, the pool widening with every second that passes.

The Operator is stunned into inaction. Fenix is gone. His friend, the one who provided support when he was alone in the badlands, has been murdered. From deep within his mind he can hear Fenix bark, but thoughts of *her* block the connection between recognition and action. Greyson reaches down and grabs the blaster from the Operator's holster before the information can process.

Bacas points his blaster at the Operator. "Put him in a cell," he orders Greyson, with his blue eyes trained on his target. "Should've listened to me instead of a dog."

Greyson rips the Operator from his chair and leads him through the door in the middle of the row of slot machines. The Operator is forced down the stairs into the darkness below, a darkness that looks a lot like the tunnels in the midline.

33

THE INTERROGATION

Claws scratch against the ground. The Operator occupies the space between a dream and the real world and can't tell from which the sound comes. His clothes stick to his skin from the moisture in the damp, musty cell.

"Fenix," he whispers. The words scratch his throat and the pain continues as each ragged breath passes in and out, in and out. His eyes open to the darkness around him. His hands are tied behind his back.

Fenix isn't here. The sound is made by the rats who have come to say hello to their newest guest. One crawls on his leg, another sniffs his head. With a kick of his leg, a rat gets thrown onto the stone floor. From then on the rodents keep their distance as they wait for him to be too weak to resist their exploration. If only they were smart enough to take orders and chew through the ropes that bind his hands.

Time gets stretched and distorted while he lies on the stone floor. He passes in and out of fitful bouts of sleep for what must amount to a full night. Sometime after he wakes up, in what he decides is morning, he sits himself up against the back wall.

The door opens and a human-shaped shadow stands in

front of the light from the hallway. The brightness hurts his eyes. He is sure that this must be a member of the gang, but which one? Whoever they are, they slide a plate across the floor towards him.

Without the use of his hands, the Operator leans forward and uses his mouth to explore the food the shadows have provided. A crust of bread and some fatty meat. Four bites and the food is gone.

"Can I have some water?" the Operator says, his voice no more than a loud whisper.

"Oh, you want water?" the shadow says. Greyson. He doesn't bother to hide the pleasure in his voice. The shadow leaves and the hall light spills full force into the cell through the open door.

Fenix barks in a space only accessible to the Operator, and the prisoner wishes he was strong enough to listen to his friend and make a run for it. Instead, all he can do is return to his seat against the back wall.

The shadow returns. "Here you go!" Greyson says.

A torrent of water hits the Operator in the face. The force knocks his head back against the wall behind him. Greyson continues to water the Operator as the prisoner loses consciousness. The last thing the Operator hears before the world fades to black is Greyson's maniacal laugh.

Rat scratches wake the Operator up again. Paws scratch his face and he shakes his head to knock them off before he sits back up. A puddle of water surrounds him and his clothes are soaked. A grumble in his stomach reminds him that he needs to eat again. Careful sweeps with his legs try to determine if there is another plate that has been left for him. His legs find nothing.

"Go away," he says to a rat who tries to climb his leg. The words don't bother his throat as much as they did the first time he woke up. He manages to bring his hands around to the front of his body by scooping them underneath his legs. His head hurts from where it struck the wall but he is able to fight through the pain and stand up. His hands search the dark room around him. Except for the metal door, the cell is made of stone. There are no handles on his side of the door. A few taps and the Operator can tell from the sound the door is thick, heavy. No chance he will be able to force his way out. He goes back to his spot against the back wall and sits down to wait.

The Operator isn't able to figure out how time works in the cell. All he knows is that sometime later the door opens and a pair of shadows approach him. They each take an arm and drag him out. The light blinds him and he can't see the two men's faces. They drag his limp body down the hall. He is thrown on the ground as they open another identical metal door down the hall. The two men pick him up, drag him into the room, and sit him in a lone chair in the middle of the room. A quick pull with a knife and the rope around his hands is cut. They tie him to the chair.

The Operator's eyes take a while to adjust to the light but, when he can see again, he sees the twins are in the room with him, one on each side of the door. This room is also made of stone and, from what he can see, is empty. The twins must appreciate the gravity of the situation because they both stare forward into the empty space of the room. Both men are silent. Their prisoner applies slight pressure to the chair beneath him, testing how secure his hands are bound to the chair. He uses his legs to lean back enough to know the chair isn't bolted to the ground. The chair is lowered too fast and the sound rings out in the room.

Both twins focus their gaze on him. "Stop moving. It won't do you any good," Dig or Doug says.

"Bacas will be here soon," says the other.

"I don't have to be tied down for him to talk to me," the Operator croaks.

Both twins fall silent and stare at the opposite wall. The Operator is surprised these two can display this level of discipline. What follows is a sense of awe for Bacas. Somehow he is able to keep these two men on a short enough leash that they can fall in line when the situation calls for it.

The door swings open and Bacas storms into the room, followed by Greyson. He walks straight to the Operator and, without a word, punches him in the face. The Operator picks his head back up in time to see the same fist strike again. Bacas doles out four more blows before Greyson hands him a towel, which the Enforcer uses to wipe the blood from his knuckles.

"Who are you?" Bacas says to the Operator.

"Nobody," the Operator says. He spits out blood, aimed at Bacas's face, but the projectile sticks to his lips and ends up on his knees.

"Lies!" Greyson yells. He raises a hand to strike the Operator but Bacas stops him before he is able to land the blow. The Operator stares at the two men, defiant.

"Look, we both know you aren't nobody," Bacas says with a calm that seems out of place. "You are somebody. Somebody that has had extensive training with a blaster while you were away from the city. Who found you? And how much did they pay you to infiltrate my operation?"

"I told you before, I am just passing through."

"I know it was them!" Bacas yells. His anger returns as quick as a thunderstorm shows up in the badlands. "What did the Sisters promise you?"

The Operator stares at Bacas. A vein pulses in the temple of the irate Enforcer. "You killed my dog," the Operator says.

"Yes I did," Bacas says. "And I will kill you too, if it's any consolation. But not until I'm done with you. Tell me about the deal you made with them."

"There is no deal. We exchanged some words over poker but that's it. You already know that."

"What did you tell them?" Bacas says.

"I told them . . ." the Operator whispers. He leans his head down and looks at the ground in front of his feet.

"Go on," says Greyson.

"I told them . . ." The Operator lifts his head and stares at Bacas. "I told them everything I will tell you! Nothing."

Bacas clenches his jaw. "Give it time. You'll change your mind." Brass knuckles emerge from his pocket and he slides his fingers into the holes. With one hand he pulls the Operator's head back by his hair and with the other he punches him in the stomach.

The prisoner strains against the hand that holds his hair as his body tries to bend over from the blow. Through watery eyes the Operator can see Bacas crack a smile. The hand that holds his hair releases and his body bends in half. At the same moment, Bacas's brass knuckles fly up from below to land an uppercut to his face.

The Operator hears a loud crack inside his skull. He flies back and the front legs of the chair leave the ground. He doesn't hear the second loud crack that fills the room as his head slams against the ground.

34

THE DOCTOR

METAL SLAMS against stone as the cell door is thrown open behind the Operator. The floor of the cell is cold and damp against the side of his head. Rat claws scurry into the shadows. His eyes are kept closed to protect them from the light. How long has it been since the interrogation? A hand grabs his shoulder and turns him onto his back. The person the hand belongs to crouches down next to him and opens his eye with clammy fingers. They inspect his pupils with a flashlight.

"He's got a concussion," the woman crouched next to him says. The Operator tries to turn his head away from the light that burns into his skull. "Hold him still," she says.

Another pair of hands covers each of his ears and squeezes his head. The woman's hands begin to feel his face. She applies slight pressure to his cheekbones and then his nose. "Broken nose too," the woman says.

"Who . . ." the Operator mutters.

"I'm a doctor," says the woman, her hands on his face.

"Look at the back of his head," Greyson says from above the Operator.

The doctor backs up and Greyson lifts the Operator to a

seated position. The doctor pulls his head down and his chin meets his chest. Her hands probe the back of his head.

"Nothing's broken," the doctor says. "But I can't tell how bad the cut is through the dried blood. Get some water so I can clean him up."

Greyson's steps echo from the hall as the man walks away. The doctor leans in close to whisper in the Operator's ear. "Bacas has my daughter. Can you kill him if I get you out of here?"

"I plan on it. He killed my dog," the Operator says through dry, cracked lips.

"Then I'd better get you healed up," she says.

Water sloshes in a bucket as it is brought back to the cell. "How long will this take? Bacas has more questions for him," Greyson says.

The doctor doesn't reply and begins to clean the back of the Operator's head. The cold water helps bring back his senses, but the increased awareness brings the pain from his head and face to the forefront of his mind.

"Give him another day before you ask any more questions," the doctor says once the blood has been washed away. "Another session like the last could kill him."

"Don't tell us what to do," Greyson says, angry at the doctor. "If Bacas wants to question him today he will."

"If you kill him you will never find your answers. Make sure you tell that to Bacas; I won't be blamed for your ignorance."

"It's his decision. Hurry up."

The doctor takes extra care wrapping the Operator's head with a bandage. She squeezes the Operator on the shoulder and helps him lie back down on the stone floor before she gets up to leave.

Rat claws on his face wake him up. How long has it been since the doctor was here? He reaches up, throws the rat off his face, and feels the bandage around his head. She wasn't a dream. He sits up against the wall and tries to look into the darkness around him. Whatever she did worked—his head doesn't throb the way it did the last time he was awake.

Now he has another reason to kill Bacas. Should he trust her? How will she help him escape? These questions float through the Operator's mind as he crawls around to feel the bottom edges of the cell, searching for the way the rats come in and out. There is nothing to find; the only entrance is through the metal door. They are trapped in here together. All he gets for his trouble are rat scratches on his hands and cracked fingernails. The Operator wipes his hands on his pants. He doesn't want to know how much rat shit is under his fingernails.

The doctor returns to the cell, followed by the twins, to check on the Operator. "You look much better," she says. She leans forward and pretends to inspect the back of his head as she whispers into his ear. "Sorry, but I need more time."

"Tell Bacas what he wants to know! If not, you will get what you deserve," the doctor says to the Operator, loud enough for the twins to hear.

She turns to the twins. "Take him to the room for questioning and let Bacas know he is ready."

The twins walk into the cell, grab the Operator, and take him to the interrogation room. He drags his feet against the floor the entire trip. The door to the interrogation room is locked. They leave him in a pile on the floor while they find the key needed to open the door.

"That one," Dig or Doug says to the other.

"No it's not. This isn't my first time!" the second twin says.

"Sure seems like it!" says the first.

The Operator opens one eye and watches the twins stare at each other, ready to fight.

The doctor has followed them to the room and steps

between the two men. "Calm down, boys, it's this one," she says. She reaches for the key ring in the hand of one of the twins and selects a black skeleton key. She slides the key into the lock and the door clicks open.

The second interrogation goes the same way as the first. Bacas wants to know who the Operator works for; the Operator replies that he was just passing through. Greyson accuses him of working for the Sisters and Bacas pulls out the brass knuckles. This time, instead of a punch to the gut and then an uppercut, Bacas hits him with a right cross.

The Operator spits out a tooth. "That all you got?" he manages to say.

Bacas gets red in the face from the jeer in front of his men. He strikes the Operator over and over as anger and frustration spill from his pores. The Operator stays conscious for the first two blows, but on the third, his chair topples over sideways and the room fades away.

35

THE SACRIFICE

"His orbital is broken," the doctor says to whoever else is also in the cell. The Operator didn't hear the cell door open or feel her inspection of his face.

"I'll collapse his face if I have to," Bacas says. Footsteps fade away as the chief Enforcer leaves the room. Outside the door, in the hall, he says, "You two, keep an eye on the doctor while she takes care of him."

The Operator is aware of every inch of his face. It's been there his entire life but now he can *feel* it. His cheeks and eyelids are swollen and painful. His hands don't have to feel the damage to know how bad it is.

The doctor takes the bandage off his head. Her fingers search the spot where his head hit the floor at the end of the first interrogation. "Completely healed. I don't understand it," she says.

"Give yourself some credit," the Operator says, the words more of an exhale than a statement. "You're good at what you do."

"It doesn't make sense," she says to herself.

"You go in, I'll stay here," Dig or Doug says to the other. The twins are the two men in the hall outside the cell.

"No. I'll stay here, you go in," the twin replies.

"I said it first! You only want to stay out here because it is the opposite of what I said." The two of them argue back and forth, each of them wanting to be the one who stands outside the cell.

The doctor leans in close to the Operator. "We are out of time. Another session with Bacas will kill you. When these two take you to the interrogation room you must make your escape."

The Operator nods.

The doctor speaks in hurried, hushed whispers. "As soon as they open the door to the interrogation room you need to push them inside and shut it. The lock to open the door from the inside is different from the one to open it from the outside. By the time these two decide which key to use you will be long gone. This is very important, so pay attention: Don't run upstairs. The only way out that way is through Suerte. No way you make it out of there alive. You have to run deeper into the crypts. At the very end is a door that leads into the midline. I've already unlocked it myself."

The doctor rubs ointment onto the Operator's wounds. "Understand?" she says.

"Yes," the Operator says through the pain of the pressure on his broken face.

The doctor wipes the leftover ointment from her hand on her shirt and stands up. "Grab him," she says to the twins in the hall from inside the cell.

They never did decide which of them would stand inside the cell. They both walk into the cell at the same time. "Get up. Time for another visit with your old buddy Bacas," Dig or Doug says to the Operator. Together, the twins hoist the Operator and drag him from the cell.

The Operator pretends to be groggier than he is and drags his feet against the ground so the twins have to work for every step they take.

"Drag your feet all you want, we don't need your help. You're getting into that room either way," Dig or Doug says.

The Operator lets his limp head bounce from side to side with each step.

Heavy breaths escape both men by the time they get to the interrogation room. They deposit him on the floor and begin to look through the ring of keys for the one they need to open the door.

"It's the black one, genius. Why do you always forget which key it is?" one twin says to the other.

"There's more than one black key on here, do you see how many there are?" Dig or Doug, whichever one has the keys in hand, says. He jiggles the ring of keys in his twin's face.

"Need my help?" the doctor says from behind the men.

"No," the twins say in unison. They focus on the door in front of them. They don't see the Operator raise himself onto one knee and prepare to pounce.

"There's only one *really* black key. Here, this one," a twin says. He grabs the ring of keys out of his brother's hand and inserts the key into the lock. The door doesn't open.

The Operator can feel Fenix with him.

"Wait, I meant this one," the twin with the keys now in hand says. He selects the black skeleton key and thrusts it into the door. A loud click and the door unlocks. Dig or Doug turns to his twin with a satisfied look on his face. "See? Told—"

Fenix begins to bark in a space only accessible to the Operator and he makes his move. The twins are driven three large steps forward. One twin trips and all three men tumble into a heap inside the room.

"Son of a bitch!" one of the twins says.

"Grab him!" says the other.

Both men reach for some part of the Operator—limbs, clothes, anything—but their hands come away empty as the Operator scrambles onto his feet and backs up. The door is slammed shut with the twins still inside. The Operator pulls the ring of keys from the door and hands them to the doctor.

"They won't be able to get out without their keys," the doctor says with a smile.

"Which way do we go?" the Operator says, his heart racing.

"Go back the way we came, then turn left. The floor slopes down, that's how you know you're going the right way," the doctor says.

"You're not coming with me?"

The doctor pulls a blaster from beneath her coat. "That's not part of the plan. Just make sure you kill Bacas, my daughter's future depends on it." She walks forward with a sense of purpose and looks around the corner ahead. She gets upset when she turns around and sees the Operator hasn't moved.

"Go! I'll hold them off as long as I can!"

Their eyes meet and the Operator hears Fenix bark from down the hall. He turns and runs to catch up to his dead dog.

36

THE ESCAPE

THE DOWNWARD ANGLE of the stone floor in the crypts isn't obvious, and if the Operator hadn't been told about the slope from the doctor, it wouldn't have registered. There are more cells than he expected and the hallway that runs between them twists and turns forever. His initial sprint slows to a jog as adrenaline wears off. When will it end? Has he run clear across to the next district? All sense of direction has been lost.

Before, and just before, his jog slows to a walk, the Operator comes to the end. The door ahead of him is made of vertical metal bars. The sound of water trickles through the spaces between the bars and mixes with the sound of his heavy breaths. The door doesn't move when pulled. A push with his shoulder does nothing either. She said it would be unlocked! Shots from a blaster are faint in the distance behind him. The Operator hopes it was the doctor who fired the shots, but now it's only a matter of time until men rush to find him.

He takes a step back and studies the door. Based on the design of the frame the door is made to be pushed. He takes a big breath and throws his full weight against the door. A loud creak echoes from the walls as the door opens a crack. Another deep breath, another push, and a bit more space opens with another loud creak. The process is repeated until there is enough space for him to squeeze through with his sore shoulder.

More blaster fire from behind. Was the creaking door loud enough to lead Bacas's men to him? Fenix barks from the midline and he begins to run towards his dog. Before turning a corner, he turns around and sees the door still open. He runs back and slams the door shut. It closes with a click and the Operator hopes that, somehow, it has locked and the men in front don't have the key.

The Operator runs for long enough that his body forces him to slow to a walk. Disoriented, he has no idea where he is. All he knows is that he needs to get far away and, somehow, make his way back to the surface. The sound of water reverberates off the walls around him as he walks. His eyes and ears are open in the darkness for a sign from the walls or from Fenix about which direction to take.

A large space opens in front of him, occupied by a body of water. Dull blue light emanates from deep below the surface and gives the whole room an eerie glow. Thirst storms to the forefront of his consciousness and he drops to his knees to drink. Before he can bring the water in his hands all the way to his mouth, he feels eyes on him through the darkness on his left. He looks at the eyes, high enough off the ground to be an adult human, as the water seeps through his fingers. The eyes don't disappear. Surrounded by darkness, the eyes reflect the blue light from the water. This far below the surface it has to be a midliner. But how are they so tall?

"Hello," the Operator says to the pair of eyes. His voice sounds harsh compared to the tranquility of the water. His hands burn. The acid rain from the surface! The deformities of the midliners must be from drinking the tainted water.

The eyes blink twice then turn away. A slow rumble fills the room. At first he thinks Bacas's men have caught up to him but, after he turns to look from where he came, he realizes the noise comes from the depths of the water. The surface of the water begins to ripple and a shadow passes through blue light.

The eyes have come back, and they stare at the Operator on the water's edge. "Can you help me?" the Operator says. Somehow he knows the eyes don't belong to someone controlled by Bacas and, odds are, they don't even know who the chief Enforcer is. The eyes dig into his soul as the rumble gets louder.

The eyes disappear into the darkness when the Operator tries to approach with his hands forward in the darkness. He tries to keep track of the exact position where he last saw the eyes. His internal compass must be miscalibrated, because he finds a stone wall ahead of him. His hands search for a way over or around the stone wall to where the eyes had been moments before. The rumble in the water gets louder. He looks into the water and a large shadow in the shape of a fish passes through the blue light.

The midliners said their friend went to talk to a fish. Did the eyes belong to the midliner who found Greyson's blaster? There are fish in the badlands who can survive on land, he's seen them himself. They are able to launch themselves from the water to grab small animals that stop to drink. Could this be one of them? Maybe a distant cousin, grown to massive proportions without any competition, who found their way in and wasn't able to find their way out.

The occasional splash joins the ripples on the surface. The Operator searches for the way over the wall with frantic sweeps of his hands. A loud splash and he turns around to see the massive head of an eyeless fish descend back into the water. He knows the fish will need more momentum. There isn't much time left.

He moves to his right and finds the opening at shoulder

height. He hoists himself up and only finds enough space for him to stand up halfway.

"This way!" he hears someone say from the far side of the water. Bacas's men have caught up to him.

The Operator wants to turn around to look at the fish, to see if it is the same kind he remembers from the badlands, but he is out of time. He begins to crawl as fast as he can. Not fast enough. Something, or someone, reaches out and grabs his leg. He struggles to free himself. It seems like he will win the battle until his captor gives a mighty tug. The Operator gets splayed out onto his belly as his leg gives out and he is dragged backwards. In desperation, he puts his leg down to stop the reversal. It works for a moment but only until another tug makes him slip on the slick rock. He puts his foot down and pushes with all his might to stand back up. The hold on his leg is released and the Operator launches himself up into the ceiling, and knocks himself out cold.

37

THE BLASTER

From the feel of the cold, hard floor against his shoulder, the Operator believes he is back in the cell. The moment lasts until his eyes open and he sees a small candle, jammed into the ground, illuminating the cement room with flickering light. More flickering light comes from another source outside the room. The room once had a door but it has been removed. His head throbs and he raises a hand to inspect the damage. Some dried blood, not much, and a large bump. He tries to piece together whatever memories he can to determine where he might be. The memory of being pulled by the leg back towards the underground lake makes him bolt upright to a seated position. Stars linger in front of his eyes from the sudden change in position.

"Where's the barking rat the others told me about?" a voice asks from the corner of the room. A midliner is crouched on all fours and the same wide eyes from the wall next to the underground lake stare at the Operator. This midliner is the same size as the other two the Operator met, but his hair has been cut short. His long, thin face reminds the Operator of Bacas.

"He's been killed," the Operator says. He looks around and sees a blaster in the corner of the room. Meat on sticks is stacked on the floor near the candle. Moldy blankets are bundled together into a makeshift pillow where his head had been moments before. "How long have I been out?"

"Not long. You struggled so much! I only wanted to show you the way out. When you tried to stand you knocked yourself out. You're taller than us, you know. And heavier."

The Operator rubs the bump on his head. "Yeah, I know. What was that thing in the water?"

"The fish without eyes. We feed her rats and she protects us. We are careful not to get too close to the water."

"The last thing I remember is trying to get away from that thing," the Operator says.

"You didn't have to worry once you were in the tunnel, she's too large to reach you in there," Usryd says. He pauses to think. "Who killed the rat?"

"Bacas."

"Did he eat it? I wonder what it tastes like . . ." the midliner says. His voice trails away as if in a dream.

"Doubt it," the Operator says, disgusted at the thought. "He will die for killing my friend."

"The rat was your friend?"

"Yes, we traveled together for a long time."

The midliner doesn't comprehend being friends with a rat, but he does understand the concept of friendship. "Then you must avenge him."

"Agreed. But he has a lot of men with him." The Operator thinks about his time in the cell. About his time in the chair. Bacas and his men need to pay for that too. "What's your name?" the Operator says.

"Usryd. The others wanted to dump your body in the

station, I had to argue to keep you here. The others don't like surface-dwellers, and two of them said you threatened to kill them."

"No, I didn't," the Operator says.

"They said you pointed your weapon at them."

"Yes, I did do that. But I didn't threaten them."

"What do you call it then? You could have killed them."

"Yes, I could have," the Operator says. The midliner has a point. "Thanks for sticking up for me, I appreciate it." He stands up and stumbles as he gets to his feet. His hand holds onto the wall for support and the stars light up in front of his eyes.

"Sit, you need to heal," Usryd says.

The Operator sits back down.

Usryd grabs the blaster from the corner and carries it over to the Operator as if the thing might go off at any moment. "This is the metal the others said you were asking about. The one that was dropped in the station. I never wanted to kill anyone so it must not work on me."

The Operator grabs the weapon, grateful to have protection back in his own hands. This has been the longest he has gone without a blaster since he went into the badlands. The blaster is government issue. A quality piece, well balanced. The Operator pulls the blaster up to chest height and looks down the sights. "If we can get this evidence to the government, Bacas will lose his top man," he says.

"One less person to kill when you take your revenge," Usryd says.

"Exactly," the Operator says. Stars cloud his vision when he aims the blaster at the candle. His eyes close as the tentacles of a headache begin to take hold. He places the blaster on the ground and uses both hands to rub his aching eyes. "I keep seeing stars," he says.

"Of course you do, it's only been a few hours since you knocked yourself out. Let your body rest until the stars stop showing up. Here, eat something," Usryd says. The midliner picks up a stick of meat and hands a roasted rat to the Operator. The hair and lips have been burned off and rodent incisors bite down on the stick that passes through its mouth.

The Operator realizes how long it has been since he has eaten anything. He uses his own two front teeth to gather flesh from outside the rodent's ribs. After dozens of small bites to get what little flesh is on the rat, the Operator looks at Usryd. "Have any water?" he asks.

Usryd hands the Operator a greasy cup, half full. Flecks of metal float in the water. After a long drink he pauses to see if he can taste the acidity that has deformed the bodies of the midliners. The water seems to taste all right and he wonders if Miguel was wrong about the acid rain on the surface. Maybe thirst caused the water to taste better than it is.

"Feel better?" Usryd asks when the cup is set down on the floor.

"Much," the Operator says.

"Lie back down and get some rest. I'll make sure the others don't kill you while you sleep."

Is this Usryd's idea of a joke? "Wait, they still want me dead? I thought you convinced them to keep me alive!"

"I did. But just because they didn't kill you *then* doesn't mean they won't change their minds. Can't believe everything people tell you," Usryd says, as if this is the most natural sentiment in the world. Is this the way all midliners think, or is it just Usryd?

"How many others are there?" the Operator asks.

"In our tribe? Twenty-two. Most of them don't want to kill you but a few can sway a lot if the matter stays unsettled. Lots of mixed feelings towards surface-dwellers."

The Operator says nothing and lays his head down on the makeshift pillow with his back against the wall. He tries to stay awake, in case the midliners come for him, but sleep drags him towards blue light that fills his dreams.

38

THE SOCIETY

THE CANDLE HAS BURNT DOWN and the room is dark when the Operator wakes up. He doesn't need to see the rest of the room to know he is alone. Thin rays of light reach the wall in front of the doorway. His hand searches the ground by his side and when the blaster is found he tucks the weapon into the waist of his pants before getting up to follow the light to its source.

The light comes from a wide tunnel bisected with two pairs of rusty rails. A group of midliners, fifteen in total, are gathered around a fire. Rats are held up for faces to eat what little meat can be found on tiny bones. All of them are too absorbed in their meal to notice the Operator. Usryd is on the left side of the fire, his face lit up by the firelight.

A female next to Usryd finishes her rat and reaches forward for another. She must feel eyes on her because she turns and faces the Operator. Her mouth falls open and a chunk of half-chewed rat flesh spills onto the floor. She picks it up, throws it back into her mouth, and stands up. She points at him but doesn't say a word.

The rest of the group turns to look at whatever startled the member of their tribe. Everyone but Usryd stands up in unison when they realize the Operator is behind them.

"Relax, it's just the surface-dweller who took the metal off our hands," Usryd says to the other midliners. "Nothing to worry about. If he wanted to do us harm he would've already done so." A roasted rat is held up to the Operator. "Want something to eat?" he says.

The Operator feels his hunger but rats take too much work for him to consider eating right now. "No thanks, I'm still full from the last one."

"Are you sure?" Usryd says while shaking the rat in his hand. "You were asleep for a long time."

"Yes, I'm sure. You shouldn't have let me sleep for so long," the Operator says. He walks closer to the fire and looks for somewhere to sit down. There are no chairs; all of the midliners sit in the bottom of their squat.

"Your body needed the rest. Do you feel better?" Usryd says.

The Operator runs through a mental checklist to take stock of the condition of his body. His hand feels for the bump on the crown of his head but it has disappeared. The stars flash in front of his eyes when he looks at the fire ahead of him. "Much," he says, determined not to acknowledge any problems in his vision. "I need to go back to the surface."

"I can show you the way," Usryd says. "You will have to be careful. A lot of men crossed the rails while you were asleep. They were on the other side for a while before they crossed back with blood on their hands."

"How long ago?"

Usryd either doesn't hear the Operator or ignores the question. Different concepts of time might not allow for the midliner to give a straight answer anyways.

Usryd finishes his meal then leads the Operator to the

station. Their approach slows as the light from the station gets larger. From behind a pillar still well within the darkness of the tunnel Usryd points to the station up ahead. "Go avenge your friend."

"I will. Thanks for everything." The Operator extends his hand and Usryd stares at it. The hand is pulled back and the Operator walks towards the light.

A dull ache behind his eyes gets worse with every step the Operator takes. He stops, leans against the side of the tunnel with his eyes closed, and waits for the pain to subside. After a few deep breaths he feels ready to continue. The ache returns as soon as his eyes open again. He pushes through and the pain goes from a mild annoyance to a deep throb. It travels from behind his eyes to the center of his skull. His eyes close again to relieve the pain.

Every time he closes his eyes the pain goes away but how can he move forward blind? If Greyson, or another one of Bacas's men, is on the ledge they will shoot him on the spot and he would never see it coming. The station is right there ahead of him when he opens his eyes but he can't keep them open for very long. Each ray of light feels like it could pierce his skull and come out through the back if he tries to ignore the pain.

Frustrated, the Operator turns around and walks back into the shadows. His eyes already feel better as he looks into the darkness. Part of him wonders if it is because he isn't used to the light, but he can't see any reason why the pain would be so intense.

Usryd hasn't moved. He watched the Operator make his way forward in fits and starts and was surprised when the Operator turned around and came back.

"What happened?" Usryd says to the Operator.

"The light," the Operator says, shaking his head. "It hurts my eyes. When I looked at the fire there were stars in my vision but now they *hurt*. Does this happen to you near the station? From all the time you spend in the dark?"

"Does what happen?"

"The light hurts your eyes."

"It doesn't hurt once we get used to it. Some stay away from the light altogether but it isn't because of the pain, they just don't want to see anyone from the surface," Usryd says. He pauses for a moment and thinks. "Your head must not be healed. Come, stay with me until it gets better."

"I don't have time! I need to know why those men crossed the midline." The Operator paces back and forth. "You said it was men who crossed the rails?"

"All men. Didn't you say the one who killed your friend keeps men with him?" Usryd says.

"Bacas. Yes, he has a lot of them."

"Then it must have been him."

"Why would all of them cross the rails?" the Operator says as he thinks out loud.

"Maybe he went to face another tribe. That's when we travel in large groups," Usryd says.

The Operator is stunned. Deep down he knew that Bacas and his men had crossed the midline to wipe out the White Jackets once and for all but he didn't want to believe it. Part of him had hoped to go to the Sisters and offer his services in exchange for the chance to kill the chief Enforcer.

"What was Bacas thinking? If the government found out . . ." the Operator says. Then again, Bacas isn't human. What could the government do to an android? How would they punish him?

"Maybe he told them a lie," Usryd says.

"What lie would he tell them?" The words don't even pass the Operator's lips before he knows who the responsibility for the murders has been pinned on: him. "My escape set all of this in motion. The reason they threw me in there in the first place is because I refused to kill them." The Operator's steps quicken as pieces begin to fall together. "He must have told them he took me into custody because I threatened to kill the White Jackets. The government probably thinks he tried to do his job by keeping me locked away. When I escaped they ended up dead anyways and he set me up to take the fall."

"He killed all of them?" Usryd says, his face covered in concern for people he has never met.

The Operator closes his eyes and exhales frustration. "Bacas is much craftier than I gave him credit for." He looks at his right hands through the shadow. "But I can be crafty too. I have the blaster . . ." He turns to the midliner. "Is it possible to have a larger fire down here? I need to train my eyes to handle more light."

"It is, but the others will consider it wasteful. Fuel is hard to come by. What about artificial light, like the kind in the station?"

"That would work, but how could I practice in there? If any of the men come into the station they will kill me."

"This isn't the only station around. There is another that nobody ever passes through. The switch still works but we never use it."

"What are we waiting for? Let's get to work."

39

THE DESERTED

THE OPERATOR and the midliner get to the other station after a long walk through the tunnels. The platforms on each side are visible shadows now that the Operator's eyes have become accustomed to the darkness. Usryd scrambles off and climbs onto the platform on their right.

"Ready?" Usryd yells out. The question echoes off the walls in the station. "Three . . . two . . ."

"Stop!" the Operator yells. His eyes are glued shut as he waits for the pain that will accompany the light. Usryd doesn't flip the switch.

The Operator takes off his shirt. "Cover the bulb with this," he says as he hands the shirt up to Usryd on the platform. "I don't want to start with the full force of the light."

Usryd covers the bulb with the shirt while the Operator stands with eyes closed. The switch is flipped and the Operator can see the red of his eyelids.

"Light's on," Usryd says.

The Operator takes an eternity to pry his eyelids apart. He takes stock of how his head feels with each additional sliver of light until his eyes are open without pain.

The abandoned station is larger than the one that separates the two rival gangs. The entrance next to Usryd is caved in with piles of cement stacked all the way to the ceiling. A paper chart on the wall, its corners curled, announces service outages. It looks like it could fall with the slightest breeze. A list of station rules hangs near the entrance next to Usryd: NO SMOKING. NO RUNNING. IF YOU SEE SOMETHING, SAY SOMETHING. The opposite entrance is blocked by a pile of furniture. Chairs, couches, and at least two tables from God knows where are all stacked on top of each other, left over from when the last train ran before the vertical revolution made horizontal travel obsolete.

The light begins to irritate the Operator's eyes, but the pain is manageable. A dull ache, not the sharp pain he experienced at the other station. Usryd, uncomfortable in the light, is much dirtier than the Operator realized. His shirt and face are covered with rat remains and his hands and feet are covered with a thick layer of dirt from walking on all fours. The midliner slinks back into the darkness of the tunnel.

"Where are you going?" the Operator says to Usryd's back.

"Back to the shadows," Usryd says as he walks on all fours towards the tunnel.

"I need your help," the Operator says. He closes his eyes and the dull ache begins to subside.

Usryd turns around, timid. "My appearance doesn't bother you?"

"Why would it? You look all right to me."

"Well, my eyes are overwhelmed. They aren't used to the light," Usryd says.

"Our eyes can learn the light together," the Operator says. "I need to practice with the blaster. Can you help me set up a target on the platform over there? I think one of those tables could work if we can pry it away from the pile," he says as he points to the entrance on the opposite side of the light source.

The two of them dismantle the pile of furniture. The work is exhausting for Usryd since he can't stand up straight and therefore can't lift anything more than three feet off the ground. It is possible for him to stand on two legs but when he does he is unable to find his balance. The table is set up on its side on the edge of the platform, but both men are too exhausted to do anything more.

"Let's go eat. We can come back after we rest so you can practice with the blaster," Usryd says.

"Agreed," says the Operator. He stands back and admires the work they have done. The pile of furniture is half as tall as it was before.

Usryd turns off the light and the Operator takes his shirt off the bulb. With his shirt back on he waits for his eyes to adjust to the darkness again before the two men head back to the rest of the tribe.

"Maybe you can teach me to shoot? I have never used the metal before," Usryd says while they walk.

"Are you sure you want to learn?"

"It won't make me want to kill, will it?"

The Operator laughs. "No, that is a choice you make yourself. Most people use them for protection."

"Okay then, I will learn. In case I have to protect the tribe."

The two men walk in silence the rest of the way. The Operator realizes his body feels good, strong. If only his eyes would work, he could go back to the surface to take his revenge. The Operator can walk faster on two legs than the midliner can on four, so every so often he has to stop and wait for the midliner to catch up before continuing.

The rest of the tribe is congregated around the fire when they return, the women and children roasting rats for the men.

The Operator and Usryd each grab a roasted rat from the pile and eat.

"Would you like another?" Usryd says with his mouth full. Grease drips down his chin and pieces of flesh stick to his face. He takes a swig of water from the cup they share to wash down the meat.

"Is that allowed?" the Operator says.

"Yes, we have done a lot of work today. We need to keep up our strength." Usryd grabs another rat from the pile and hands it to the Operator. "Here, eat."

The Operator takes the rat and sets to work on his second. His thirst is powerful but since he suspects the acidic water is responsible for the deformities of the midliners he only allows himself small sips from the cup he shares with Usryd. He tries to convince himself the tainted water is only harmful during midliner development but, even with this rationalization in mind, he doesn't drink as much as he would like. In the badlands he never had enough water to drink either.

Shadows cast into the surrounding tunnels lengthen as the fire dies down. The dull ache behind the Operator's eyes combined with a full stomach provide the ingredients for sleep. Usryd sinks lower and lower, his eyelids on the same trajectory, until the midliner abandons his efforts to stay upright and lies down. Slow, steady breaths emanate from Usryd as he sleeps. The Operator isn't as comfortable as the midliner among the rest of the tribe. He goes back to the room where he first woke up, determined to find darkness and give his eyes their needed rest. When he gets to the room he collapses onto the pile of rags that serves as a pillow.

Usryd crawls into the room sometime in the middle of the night and lies down to sleep by the Operator's feet. The Operator dreams Fenix has come back to help him take his revenge.

40

THE PRACTICE

Usryd shakes the Operator awake. "Did you want to eat before we go? The rats have just been cooked," he says.

It takes the Operator a moment to remember where he is. The candle is lit and the midliner's face is inches from his own. "Yes," he says, once the awareness of his situation returns. He sits up. "How are there so many rats to eat?"

"The men spend all day gathering them," Usryd says.

"I didn't see any when we were walking yesterday."

"They try and hide but if you know where to look they are easy to catch."

The Operator reaches up, stretches out. "On the surface they walk the streets with the people."

"The surface people don't appreciate what they have. They think they are too good to eat rats," Usryd says, with disdain heavy in his voice.

The midliner leads the Operator to the fire, where they each consume a rat for breakfast. The light from the fire doesn't affect the Operator's eyes and he is hopeful that today will be better than the last.

When they get to the station both he and Usryd climb onto

the platform. The Operator again covers the bulb with his shirt before Usryd flips the switch. The light hurts worse than the Operator remembers. He turns his back to the bulb and faces the side-lying table on the opposite platform. Without direct exposure to the rays of light his eyes don't experience the same pain, but he still needs to shut them every so often in order to let them rest.

The Operator, his eyes open, draws his blaster, squints down the sights, and tries to ignore the ache. He aims for the center of the table and squeezes the trigger. A black dot appears on the table to the right of center, off the mark by the length of his forearm.

"Is that where you aimed?" Usryd says.

"No," the Operator says. He doesn't want to talk about it. If he were on the surface he would be embarrassed by how bad the shot was. He focuses on the center of the table again and fires. The shot is overcorrected. It hits to the left of the center, closer than before but still not on target. The dull ache builds as he takes aim a third time. His eyes need to close, to relieve the pain, but he is determined to hit the center. His third shot finds the center of the table. Higher than he had aimed by the length of a hand but in the center nonetheless.

His eyes close and he waits for the pain to subside.

"Can I try?" Usryd says.

The Operator hands the midliner the blaster and Usryd does his best to mimic the Operator's actions. His posture makes it hard for him to get the gun parallel to the ground with his arm straight and he struggles to get the gun high enough to take proper aim.

"You said you've never shot before?" the Operator asks.

"Not yet," Usryd says as he pulls the trigger. A black spot shows up two feet below the lip of the platform, not even close to the table.

"Keeping your arm straight is going to be a problem," the Operator says. "You will need to keep a bent elbow. Not impossible to shoot this way but it will make it harder to aim. Make sure you focus on the target."

Usryd raises the gun with a bent arm. The Operator takes hold of the barrel of the weapon and points it in the general direction of the table. "Now stare at the spot you want to hit," he says.

Usryd fires, and evidence of the shot appears three feet to the right of the table.

"Closer, at least you were on the same level as the table this time. Make sure you exhale before you shoot and only use your finger to squeeze the trigger. Looks like you pulled the blaster to the right because you used your whole hand on the last shot."

Usryd nods and stares at the table. A long exhale and a squeeze of the trigger. The shot hits the top of the table to the right of center.

"You see that? I hit it!" Usryd says.

"I saw," the Operator says. He takes the blaster from Usryd. "Let me get some shots in."

The two of them trade off turns with the blaster for the next few hours. The Operator gets to the point where he can hit the center every time with the low level of light in the room. Not without pain—he still needs to close his eyes every few shots—but he can keep his eyes open longer with time. Usryd manages to hit the table a handful of times, but his bent elbow makes his accuracy erratic. He tries his hardest to focus on the target, but multiple times he gets so frustrated that he hands the blaster back to the Operator after one shot so he can sit to the side and sulk. The Operator ends the day by shooting with his shirt back on and the bulb exposed. The ache sits behind his eyes, but he is able to get one shot off before he has to close them to relieve the pain.

The next day the two men come back and practice again. The Operator is able to hit the center of the target without the shirt on the bulb twice before the pain becomes unbearable. By the end of the second day Usryd is able to hit the table with half of his shots. Their training continues for days on end. Eventually, the Operator is able to hit the center of the table six times before he needs to close his eyes.

"I wonder if Stim would help with the pain," the Operator says to Usryd with his eyes closed. The midliner fires a shot and the Operator can hear the shot hit the table. Most of Usryd's shots hit the table. Now the midliner works on making sure each shot hits the same spot.

"Stim? What's that?" Usryd says. He fires again.

"Stim amplifies focus and stamina. Normal people become highly skilled and highly skilled people become unstoppable. It's what the Enforcers use to control the people on the surface."

"If it would help with my accuracy I wouldn't mind trying some myself," Usryd says.

"It definitely would. It's hard to miss when you're stimmed," the Operator says.

"Maybe it would help with your pain."

"I haven't taken any in a long time. There's no point in considering it, Bacas controls all the Stim in the district. It was just a thought," the Operator says.

"Why haven't you taken any?" Usryd says. He fires another shot.

"Just decided not to. If I'm not good enough without it then I deserve to die."

"But other people use it, right?"

"Yes."

"So you are at a disadvantage without it?"

"Correct."

"Sounds like you have a death wish," Usryd says. He hands

the blaster back to the Operator.

"Let's switch platforms. I want to shoot into the light."

Usryd looks around. "There isn't anything to shoot over here."

"That's fine, I'll pick a spot on the wall," the Operator says. The two of them walk across to the opposite side of the station and face the light.

The dull ache turns into a searing pain as the Operator looks into the light. He tries to focus past the pain but the knives in his eyes won't let themselves be ignored. The pain goes away once his eyes are closed. In the darkness he hears Fenix bark. Inspired by his dog, the Operator lifts the blaster without opening his eyes. After a long exhale, he opens his eyes, finds his target, and takes his shot. There is no room for hesitation because the pain returns right away. His eyes snap shut.

"Where did the shot hit?" the Operator asks Usryd.

"You hit a piece of paper with words on it."

The Operator flashes his eyes open and sees his shot hit the exact spot he had aimed for. "That's where I was aiming. It's a good start but there is no way I will be able to take that much time for each and every shot on the surface. I thought I was closer to being ready to go back but it looks like my eyes have a different idea."

The Operator hands the blaster to Usryd. "What should I aim for?" the midliner asks.

"Pick out different spots on the wall and hit them. You have done well hitting the table but now you need to learn to line up multiple shots."

"I can see how this can get complicated," Usryd says. He squeezes the trigger. "Imagine if these were moving!"

"Yes, imagine . . ." the Operator says. The androids in Sigma moved. Bacas will move. It's only a matter of time before he makes his move onto the surface.

41

THE HUNTED

THE OPERATOR WARMS UP for target practice with the light behind him. Shots bury themselves in the table and he doesn't have to see where they land to know each one is on target. Ten shots are fired before the dull ache creeps into his head. His eyes close and he waits for the pain to subside before he switches sides to shoot into the light. Two shots into the light are taken, both on target, before his eyes need to rest. A countdown from five is all the time it takes for the pain to go away. A rhythm emerges: two shots then countdown, two shots then countdown.

Usryd has become a more consistent marksman. Not good, but better. Each shot is called out before it is taken and the midliner smiles when the black mark shows up less than a forearm's length away from the center of each target.

"We need to tighten that spread. Your shots should be close enough to the center that your hand could cover them all," the Operator says to his pupil.

"I'm trying, but my back gets tired from being upright and my shots get pulled off target," Usryd says.

"There's no room for excuses when your life's on the line," the Operator says. His eyes close to take a break from the light.

"Why would my life be on the line?" says Usryd, worried.

"You never know," the Operator says. "Now focus."

The Operator's eyes get accustomed to the direct brightness from the bulb. He is able to get six shots off before he has to close his eyes, as long as those six shots are fired in quick succession. In order to hit multiple targets he has to look at them, close his eyes, visualize the plan, and fire the second his eyes open again. The countdown from five numbs the pain enough for him to practice this sequence multiple times.

"I never thought my head would take this long to heal," the Operator says as he walks back to the fire with Usryd after another day of practice.

"Didn't you say you also hit your head before the tunnel?" Usryd says.

"Yes, I did."

"That's a lot in a short time. Nobody heals right away," says Usryd.

"I should," the Operator says with a smile. "Can you lead me to the surface? I think I can handle myself well enough now."

"What about all those men?" Usryd says.

"I won't go to their side. I want to go to the side they attacked, see if I can find out what has happened while I've been down here."

After another meal of roasted rat, the two marksmen make their way to the station that splits the district between the Sisters and Bacas. As the Operator approaches, he can feel the dull ache behind his eyes return but, this time, it doesn't get worse with every step. At the edge of the station, still covered in shadow, he confirms that as long as he closes his eyes every so often he can handle the light.

The station is deserted. The Operator climbs onto the platform on the Sisters' side with his attention on the opposite side of the station. Sunlight spills into the station from the stairs that lead up to the surface. Not a lot, because of the haze, but enough to bother his eyes in a way he didn't experience underground. The pain increases with every step he takes towards the stairs that lead to the Sisters. "No way," he says to the air around him. With his eyes closed he performs his countdown before he tries to continue to the stairs through the pain. The pain becomes so intense that he has to stop and lean against the wall with his eyes closed, an easy target if anyone were to walk into the station on the far side. He turns around and goes back.

"The sunlight brings the pain back," he tells Usryd when he gets into the tunnel. The darkness is a welcome break for his eyes.

"Then wait for the darkness," Usryd says.

"Looks like I have to. I thought my eyes were better than this."

"The injuries were worse than you thought. This is what happens when you don't take care of yourself!"

"Bacas will pay for this," the Operator says.

Usryd leads the Operator back to the station once night has fallen in the city. The Operator walks through the deserted station to the city streets on his way to the Sisters. The artificial light cast down from the buildings causes the expected dull ache behind his eyes to persist, but the perpetual haze mutes the intensity. He sticks to the shadows between buildings as he passes through the streets. Nobody is out, and anyone who looks down and sees him from their window might get suspicious. He stands tall and pretends to belong. The main intersection is up ahead, illuminated by the floodlight where the three White Jackets stood the last time he was here. The space beneath the light is empty.

At the corner of the intersection he peeks around the building and sees the entrance to the tavern, illuminated by its faded neon sign. Two guards are posted outside the door but neither have White Jackets on. After a big breath the Operator embarks down the strip of shops with his eyes closed. His countdown is performed while he walks.

"Hey! You there! What are you doing out?" one of the guards yells when they spot him.

The Operator's heartbeat remains steady and he opens his eyes.

The second security guard turns around with a choppy twist and opens the door behind him. "We need a team outside, somebody's out past curfew!" the man yells into the tavern. Something seems off about his voice. The words are correct but the spaces between each word don't seem quite right . . .

Androids. An older model, based on their speech. Durable.

The Operator darts into a side street and begins to run. Curfew? The Sisters must be dead or have been taken prisoner, because they would never allow a curfew on their side. Footsteps pound the cement behind him, urging his legs to run faster. Two androids aren't a problem, but how many androids comprise the team that's been called for? His hand grasps the blaster at his side and he begins to look for cover, somewhere he can set up and shoot the heads off his pursuers. A metal drum would be perfect, but the rusted car ahead will have to do.

A female voice reaches his ears when he gets behind the car, before he can turn around and take aim. "This way," she says. The woman is in the alley behind him. A white scarf covers her head. She beckons with her hand for him to follow.

The Operator trusts her without a second thought. He blinks often while he runs so the pain in his eyes doesn't become unbearable and almost misses her plunge through a side door. The Operator follows the white scarf and finds himself in front of a set of stairs that can be taken up or down. Footsteps ring out from the stairs above. He clears two steps at a time on the way up. The door to the second floor swings closed and he rushes through to the hall on the other side. The tail of her scarf turns the corner ahead of him. When he turns the corner himself, he is stopped dead in his tracks by a group of seven women, six of them White Jackets. All of them have weapons drawn. His hand hovers over the blaster at his side.

"Don't even think about it. There's no way you could take all of us out no matter how good you are," the woman with the white scarf says. The Operator recognizes the sharpness in her voice. Klepsydra.

The Operator puts his hands up, closes his eyes, and counts backwards from five. "What happened to the rest of you?" he says when his eyes open again.

One of the White Jackets speaks up. "Bacas. He thought we helped you hide. When he couldn't find you he killed the others, hoping you'd give yourself up. They didn't stand a chance."

Another White Jacket can't control herself any longer. "It's all your fault! They wanted you!" she says with tears in her eyes.

"Keep your mouth shut," Klepsydra says to her comrade.

"I'm sorry, I didn't know," the Operator says to the distraught woman.

"Where were you?" another woman asks.

"After I escaped from Bacas I hid in the midline," he says.

"Bacas told the government you killed the rest of us. All three districts are looking for you," Klepsydra says. The scarf is still around her head.

The Operator doesn't want her to know that he knows her identity. "Great. I should've stayed in the midline," he says.

"Put your blasters away," Klepsydra says. The other women look in horror as she takes the scarf off to expose her face.

"They didn't get you yet. Why am I not surprised?" the Operator says with a smirk.

"Come," the Sister says.

The White Jackets part as Klepsydra leads the Operator through a door down the hall. The room is large and there are blankets all over the floor. "We move every night so they don't find us," Klepsydra says.

"Can you help me get back to the midline?" the Operator says.

"The midline? No, we need your help to get rid of these thugs!"

"You and I both know that even if we were able to kill the men here there are many more who will come to take their place. I need to go back to the midline, cross, and kill Bacas."

The women all stare at the Operator.

"Your plan is to kill Bacas? Alone?" Klepsydra says.

"Alone. He killed my dog."

"Let us help you. Bacas took away our family."

"Let us help!"

"Please!"

"No," the Operator says with finality. The women get quiet. "Get me to the midline, I will take care of him myself. Once he is gone, you can go live on his side. These men won't think to search for you over there."

"You can't stop us from helping you kill him," Klepsydra says. Her demeanor ices over. "What if we decide not to help you get to the midline?"

"You're right, I can't stop you. I'm asking you to trust me. I have a plan."

"Iris trusted and look where that got her!" a White Jacket says. She turns around with her hands over her face.

Klepsydra studies the Operator's face. "You think you can do this?" she says.

"I know I can."

Klepsydra sends two White Jackets to escort the Operator

through the buildings and back to the station. The curfew doesn't affect their group in any meaningful way since they have access to every building below the reclaimers and get around the city through the network of connections between them. The first rays of sunlight enter the city as they exit through a door right next to the stairs that descend to the station.

"Come over tomorrow morning. They will all be dead by then," the Operator says.

"And what if they kill you? We will be walking to our deaths," a White Jacket says.

"I'm sure you can figure out a way to check if Bacas has been killed or not. I'll leave that up to you."

The Operator runs down the stairs, two at a time, his eyes closed to stop the sunlight's knives from piercing his skull.

42

THE TRADE

"Knew you couldn't stay away forever," Ludavico says from the other side of the station. He stands tall on the opposite platform, proud, his blond hair peeking through the bandage around his head and his blaster aimed at the Operator.

The Operator is frozen in place. His hands reach up even though he isn't one hundred percent sure Ludavico could hit him from this distance. The fact that Ludavico is able to aim at him without moving means he isn't stimmed and, if not, how good is his accuracy? The Operator doesn't want to find out.

"You love to stick your nose in other people's business," Ludavico says, loud enough for the sound to travel across the station. "It's in your nature. I could tell from the first time I saw you when you came into the city with your annoying mutt."

The Operator's blood boils. He closes his eyes and counts down from ten, this time to calm himself as well as rest his eyes. "What does Bacas want from me?" he says when his eyes open.

"Nothing you can give him, other than your life. He's become obsessed with finding you ever since you escaped. He has tried to piece together your history. To figure out where you came from, where you went in the badlands. You are his mystery, one he intends to solve even if he has to pull scraps of information out of you piece by piece."

"He will die for killing my dog," the Operator says.

"What? Speak up, I can't hear you!" Ludavico says.

"He killed my dog! He has to die."

"So he killed your mutt? Boo-hoo! Are you going to go to war with him? With us? Manolo told me how you shoot. Said he has never seen anything like it. The twins are downright terrified Bacas will order them to kill you if you come back. Me, I guess I am lucky I was unconscious because I have no fear of you whatsoever." He fires a shot that hits the ground next to the Operator's feet.

The Operator doesn't move, doesn't even blink. He stares at Ludavico. "If I have to kill every one of you I will. Bacas killed Fenix. I can't let that go."

"There are too many of us, even for you. Were you on your way over right now?" Ludavico says.

"No." The Operator closes his eyes. He imagines how good it would feel, will feel, to take his revenge. Too bad the sun keeps him away from the surface during the day or else he would shoot his way past Ludavico and through the rest of the gang right now.

Rays of light trickle into the station. The Operator can't keep his eyes open as long as he could a few minutes ago. He tries to focus on Ludavico, to ignore the pain behind each eye, but his eyes close on their own. When he opens them again he watches Ludavico raise his blaster away from the floor and line up his shot. Would the blond man be able to hit his head from this far away? He has to close his eyes again. A shot rings out and hits the wall behind him. When his eyes open he sees Ludavico put his blaster away.

"You saved my life," Ludavico says. "Now we are even. When you come for your revenge I won't miss." Ludavico turns and walks back to the steps that lead up to the surface. He sits down on the bottom step and watches the Operator walk into the tunnels.

Usryd has watched the whole exchange from the darkness of the tunnel. "He didn't even care that you had a blaster too!" the midliner says. "What if you decided to pull your own weapon when his back was turned? He wasn't even looking! You should have done it. One less person to shoot through later."

"I couldn't do that."

"Why not? If I had a blaster I would have shot him for you from in here," Usryd says as the two of them begin to walk back to the rest of the tribe.

"Don't worry, I'll kill him later."

"I don't get it," Usryd says. "He'll die regardless, what does it matter when it happens?"

"Things are different on the surface. You don't have to understand, you aren't the one who will pull the trigger."

Usryd stays silent until the two men get back to the fire. "Are you hungry? We have meat." They each grab a rat and begin to eat. The Operator looks around the fire and sees the rest of the tribe watch him take each bite, their eyes full of hostility. How many rats has he eaten without adding any more to their stock?

The Operator tells Usryd about what happened on the surface, how outsiders have taken control of the Sisters' district and killed most of the White Jackets.

"Didn't you say the blaster could get the man with Bacas in trouble?" Usryd says when the Operator finishes his story.

"Greyson? Yes, but we would also need the memory of someone who saw the murders. If not, Greyson could claim the weapon was used in self-defense."

"How would you get a memory?"

"A machine scans the brain and recreates the images on a screen. All the person would have to do is think about what they saw."

"Does it hurt?" Usryd asks. He wraps his arms around his knees and gives them a squeeze. The rest of the midliners watch with curiosity as the two men talk.

"From what I understand, no, but I've never had it done to me. My friend throws memories on the screen with no problem at all."

"But I, someone, would have to go to the surface?"

"Yes, the extraction would have to be performed on the surface." The Operator looks at Usryd. "Did you see what happened?"

An older female midliner nudges Usryd with her elbow. "Shut your mouth if you want to stay alive," she says, with no attempt to keep the warning between the two of them.

"Don't worry," Usryd says to her. "Our friend here is going to kill them all anyways. I won't have to go to the surface because nobody will be left alive to get in trouble." Usryd turns to the Operator. "Right?"

"That's right." The Operator says. The government needs to know the kinds of people Bacas employs if, for some reason, they kill him before he is able to kill them all. Is there any way for him to introduce Usryd to Klepsydra so she could get the memory if his attack fails? The memory should provide enough evidence against Greyson even without the blaster the Operator will have with him if he dies. Would it be possible to extract his own memories after death? The government should know about the human version of Bacas that was killed in Sigma. Do they know this version of Bacas is an android?

The Operator decides to kill everyone first, then clear his name after the fact.

"The people would stare at you, Usryd," the older midliner says.

"Why would they stare?" Usryd asks.

"Because of the way you look. That's why nobody goes into the light. They treat us like freaks."

"No, we don't go into the light because we crave the freedom of the tunnels."

"Running around in dark tunnels and eating rats seems free to you?" another midliner says from across the fire.

"There are many things you don't understand," the female midliner tells Usryd.

Usryd hangs his head, gets up, and walks away from the fire.

The Operator doesn't want to stay in his seat at the edge of the fire without his friend. He goes back to the dark room to sleep the day away. He hopes that, with his eyes shut for so long, the pain will stay away on the surface long enough for him to kill Bacas's men as fast as he killed the androids in Sigma.

Sleep arrives in between thoughts about how Bacas's men might not be men at all, and how history will repeat itself tonight.

43

THE EMERGENCE

"It's dark on the surface. Time to go," Usryd says.

"Okay, okay, I'm up," the Operator says. He sits up. Dead to the world, he didn't hear Usryd walk into the room. "How long have I been out?" He forces his eyes open wider than normal in an effort to wake himself up.

"A long time, the sun has been down for a while. You must have needed the rest."

"You should have woken me up as soon as it went down!" The Operator scrambles to get himself together. The process doesn't take long; all he has to do is throw his jacket on and grab the blaster.

"I didn't know how long you wanted to sleep!" Usryd says in defense of his inaction. "You never told me to wake you up."

"You knew I had to get going," the Operator says, annoyed.

"How do you feel?" Usryd says.

"I feel like killing Bacas."

The Operator walks behind Usryd to the station. Part of him wonders if Ludavico has set a trap for him on the surface. The more he thinks about it, the more he comes to believe there is no way Ludavico would be able to tell Bacas about the Operator without the Enforcer finding out Ludavico let the Operator escape into the tunnels. If the blond man values his life he would make sure to stay far away from the station. Those closest to the station will be the first ones killed.

The station is deserted. The Operator climbs onto the platform and takes one last look at Usryd standing in the shadows of the tunnel. Without a word of goodbye he walks the length of the platform, the window to the hoarder's room where he and Miguel watched the murders on his left. He wonders if anyone in the windows has their eyes on him.

No welcome party on the surface. Are the streets empty because the people in the city know what is about to happen? Maybe some of them sense the impending danger and stay away without knowing why. A light rain falls through the haze. The reclaimers must need to be emptied but, with the White Jackets deposed, who is charged with the task?

The Operator stays close to the buildings in order to shield himself from the acidic rain. Fenix should be with him. The dog always knew when it was time to shoot and when is was time to wait and see what develops. Will the memory of Fenix still be able to tell him when to start shooting even though he has been murdered? The Operator knows he can't rely on it. His own instincts will have to be responsible for telling him when to begin killing everyone who stands in his way. The weight of the decision of when to flip the switch is heavy on his mind.

Two men walk out of an alley ahead of him and the Operator places his hand around the grip of his blaster at his side, ready to draw. For a split second he thinks they will address him, tell him to stay where he is while they approach, but they both turn towards the intersection without a second thought to the man on the street with them at this late hour. He dips into the alley to close his eyes and perform the countdown in order to make sure the ache in his eyes doesn't return before the action begins.

There are no signs the gang knows he is on his way. The lights of the bazaar in the intersection shine bright, and streaks of light extend out from each source, the rays trapped by the weather. He steps into another alley to rest his eyes again. Rats are everywhere. He is amazed at how many rats are on the surface after he saw none during his time in the tunnels. How are the midliners able to find and kill enough to feed themselves?

The crowd of people in the bazaar materializes through the gloom as he walks towards them. He walks until he is right outside the cover of the canopy and scans the faces beneath. Multiple pairs of Bacas's men patrol the bazaar. Two of them walk along the right side of the covered intersection. If they continue on their path they will approach him head-on. The Operator draws his blaster and sits down with his back against the building. He crosses his arms and hides the weapon inside his jacket. His head hangs down and he pretends to be asleep. Water collects in his hair and trickles to the ground from his forehead.

"Hey you!" a voice calls out.

Heavy footsteps splash through water on their approach to the Operator, but he doesn't move. His eyes are closed and his breathing steady as he takes advantage of the time before the shoot-out begins. The two men stop right next to him. The Operator opens his eyes, his head still down, and sees two pairs of boots. A hand reaches down and shakes his right shoulder. "Wake up," they tell him. He doesn't move.

"Wake. Up!" the second man says as he kicks the Operator's boot. The hand of the first shakes the Operator's shoulder again.

Deep within his mind the Operator can hear Fenix bark. In a flash he reaches his left hand up to the hand on his right shoulder and pulls the man headfirst to the ground. In the same movement he pulls the blaster up and shoots the second man twice, the first time in the stomach and the second time in the head. The first man is about to get off the ground and attack when he is shot in the face.

The Operator stands up, cracks his neck, and wipes the rain from his coat. People in the crowd look at him for an instant before they turn away, intent on going about their own business. He surveys the crowd to locate the rest of the men who will need to be eliminated before he can advance to Bacas. There are six more groups of two: four pairs in the crowd and two pairs under the floodlight to the left of the bazaar, on the street to Suerte. The Operator stands tall and, after a long exhale, he inserts himself into the crowd of people and heads towards a food cart on the right side of the bazaar. He locates a pair of gang members who approach from the far side of the intersection. They are busy in conversation and don't pay attention to a single person around them. The Operator turns his back to them and pretends to inspect the food on the cart, fluff pastries filled with unidentified meat. His head is kept down, and through his peripherals he sees the two men pass behind him from left to right. The Operator turns to his right and pulls his blaster level with their skulls. Two quick shots and two bodies crumple to the ground in front of him.

The crowds fall silent as they create a circle around the corpses. The Operator backs into the crowd and looks for his next two victims.

Two men jostle past him from behind and rush to the side of the corpses. One of them kneels on the ground to check if either man is still alive. When he confirms they are both dead the man stands up and scans the crowd. The Operator keeps his head bent, his face hidden, as he walks forward through living bodies.

Once he is certain nobody in the crowd is in the way, he raises his blaster and fires two more shots.

Four bodies are now on the ground, each one with a single shot through their skulls.

By now everyone in the crowd realizes the man in the duster has killed the gang members and they widen the circle to include him as well. He walks behind the food cart and squats down with his back against the square bottom. He closes his eyes and counts backwards from five.

"You've come back," he hears a voice call out.

"Won't you come out and play?" another man says from behind him on his right. Ludavico.

"Bacas just wants to talk," he hears a third man say from his left. There must be two pairs of men, one on each side of the cart. The Operator takes a deep breath, drives his legs into the ground, and pushes on the cart. The legs on the side of the cart against his back raise off the ground before he lets them fall back to their original position. With a substantial push, the cart topples over. His back stays glued to the side and the cart hits the ground with the Operator on top, already turning to his left. He fires two quick shots and rolls to his left for cover against the men on his right. The two gang members on the left double over from the shots they took in the stomach. As soon as the Operator hits the pavement, two more shots find the heads of the two bent-over gang members.

The Operator stays curled up with his back to the cart, hidden from the shots that pour in from Ludavico and his counterpart. They shoot for so long and with no break that the Operator realizes their plan is to shoot through the cart, no matter how long it takes. It won't take very long. The Operator turns around to face the cart and adjusts himself so he can see the foot of one shooter in the space between the cart and the ground. He takes aim, hits the foot, and a large hole opens below the ankle of the unfortunate victim. With a scream, the man falls on the ground. The Operator fires again and this time finds his left wrist.

The gang member writhes in pain on the ground, the ends of his leg and arm mangled masses of flesh. He crawls backwards on knees and elbows in an attempt to get away from shots that come from ground level.

"I'll kill you!" Ludavico says.

From the location of his voice the Operator knows the blond man is the one still standing.

Ludavico jumps onto the food cart. "Bacas will give me a big reward for this," he says to the air around him.

The Operator visualizes his next move. He spins around to reposition himself with his feet against the cart, the two dead bodies behind the crown of his head. Both hands grasp the grip of his blaster. At the first sight of blond hair over the edge of the cart he kicks his legs out with all of his strength. The cart shifts, and the Operator slides backwards against the pavement. Ludavico stumbles, and in the same instant the Operator fires a shot that lands right below blond hair. Ludavico falls to a heap on top of the cart and the Operator stands up.

The man who has lost the use of one hand and one foot tries to crawl even faster now that he is the last man alive. "Please," he says, tears running down his cheeks.

The Operator stares at the man on the ground as he tries to get away. Fenix barks and the Operator fires. Blood mixes with tears as they both flow from the dead man's face.

44

THE DISSECTION

THE CROWD SCATTERS. Through the fleeing bodies the Operator sees the four men between the bazaar and Suerte, the floodlight above illuminating one pair of faces. The twins. Even from across the intersection he can tell they are arguing. The other two faces are still hidden in shadow. With any luck one of them is Greyson. All four men withdraw something from their pockets and stab themselves in their forearms. Stim. These last four should be fun.

The Operator raises his blaster and aims at the twins, but he doesn't plan to shoot with so many people still between them. Those who remain between the Operator and his targets realize what is about to happen and scramble to get out of his way. The threat of the shot spreads into the crowd, and a wedge is created that begins at the Operator and ends with its point at the floodlight. The dull ache returns behind the Operator's focused eyes.

The shot from the Operator's blaster passes right by the head of the last member of the crowd to move out of the way and lands in Dig or Doug's left eye. The Operator shakes his head. The shot was supposed to hit between the twin's eyes. A moment's hesitation about why the shot missed its target gives the other twin enough time to take cover behind a food cart at the edge of the bazaar.

The other pair of men take cover behind a rusted-out car on the far side of the street. The road to Suerte now passes through Bacas's men.

The Operator fires continuous shots at the rusted-out car as he runs forward, hopeful that the twin stays behind the food cart long enough for his plan to work. The shots, not meant to kill, are meant to pin the two men down. With a full head of steam, the Operator slams his shoulder into the food cart. It topples over and lands on top of Dig or Doug, which-ever one is still alive. A scream rings out as the twin is pinned underneath.

The Operator turns to face the rusted skeleton of a car and pours more shots into the side while he backs away. The second twin tries to wriggle himself free from under the cart, his chest against the ground and his upper torso exposed. The Operator takes a one-shot break between shots at the rusted car to hit the twin in the back of the head.

Neither man behind the cover of the car has shown any part of their body. Maybe they wait for a break in the downpour of shots or maybe they have their blasters aimed to the sides, one left and one right, as they wait for the Operator to show himself around one side. The Operator allows himself a smile as he runs to where they hide while continuous shots emanate from his weapon. With a leap, the Operator is on top of the car, his blaster pointed down at two heads. Both men tilt their heads back, mouths agape, as the Operator takes aim. Two shots and the two men join the others in the afterlife. Blood from the four bodies outside the protection of the canopy mixes with rain and streams into the city the same way the crowds streamed away from the shoot-out.

The Operator looks around with his back to the car to

double-check there are no other men who need to be killed. The streets are deserted other than the bodies of the twelve men.

Suerte is up ahead. No guards stand outside, but there are people passed out against the buildings on each side. Are any of them Bacas's men, pretending to be asleep to trick him the same way he tricked the first two gangsters? The Operator's head is on a swivel as he waits for any one of them to make a move.

The Operator stands outside the door and closes his eyes for a long countdown, all the way from ten, in order to rest his eyes. The bright lights inside Suerte make him wary. He crouches down and pushes the door open, careful not to rush in, in case Bacas has laid a trap for him inside. The blaster is pointed forward and searches for members of the gang to appear as more of the room is exposed.

Three members of Bacas's gang are focused on the door, but all three of them are shot in the head before they can get their own shots off.

"Shoot him!" Greyson yells from somewhere inside. Shots ring out against the metal door. The Operator can feel the force of each shot hit the door through his shoulder. Some of the shots hit the wall next to the door as gang members try to shoot into the widening gap between the door and the wall. The shots continue as the door creeps open like the minute hand of a clock, too slow for anyone to be aware but forever marching on. Two members of Bacas's gang are exposed as the door opens but neither of them expect the Operator to be crouched. Both men have their heads collected.

There is a sudden push from the other side of the door and the Operator almost loses his balance. His foot finds the threshold of the door and he is able to stop his backwards slide.

"I knew you would come back," Greyson says from the other side of the door.

"I came back to kill each and every one of you," the Operator says.

"Even if you manage to kill me you won't be able to kill Bacas. He is better than you. Much better. The others might believe you can match his skill but I know better, I've seen it in your eyes. The hesitation. The inability to do what needs to be done. You aren't cut out to make the difficult decisions. The most you will ever be is a follower."

"What does that make you, Greyson?" The Operator pushes against the threshold with his foot and the door begins to creep open. He closes his eyes to give them a moment's rest while Greyson pushes back in a fight for his life.

Greyson isn't the only gang member left alive in the casino. The last of Bacas's men becomes inspired and jumps into the space of the open door. He takes wild shots and one of them hits the Operator in the arm. The Operator opens his eyes, raises his blaster through the pain, and takes aim. His shot hits the man right between the eyes and gives death yet another gift.

With one final heave the Operator throws the door wide open. The Operator keeps his eyes open through the dull ache that persists, and he looks for any other members of the gang who have managed to stay alive. Everyone is dead in the casino except Greyson behind the door. Bacas is nowhere to be found. A hand shoots past the door as it reaches for a blaster on the ground. One quick shot and the hand has a hole through the center of its palm.

"Where's Bacas?" the Operator says. He holds the blaster in his left hand and closes the door with his right.

Greyson turns onto his back and props himself on one elbow, his furious eyes on the Operator. He says nothing.

"Where's Bacas," the Operator says again.

Greyson spits on the Operator. He had aimed for the Operator's face but there was only enough power for the spit to land on the Operator's chest.

The Operator aims his blaster at Greyson's head. "I'm not going to ask you again," he says. He lowers the blaster down, first to Greyson's chest, then to his knee. He fires and Greyson cries out in pain.

Greyson turns on his side and pounds his fist into the ground. "Bacas will kill you!" he says through gritted teeth.

"You're a dead man. Might as well tell me where he is," the Operator says.

"Ask Miguel," Greyson says.

The Operator's stomach drops to the floor. "Bacas is at the pool hall?"

"Has been for a few days now. He's convinced the owner knows where you went. At first the man wouldn't talk, but Bacas has his ways. It took Miguel a while, but in the end he did tell us everything he knows. It wasn't much. Bacas is still there punishing him for helping you in the first place."

The Operator squints through painful eyes and takes his final aim. Their eyes meet. Greyson understands what is about to happen and closes his eyes to wait for the inevitable. The Operator squeezes the trigger and whatever is left of Greyson's head hits the floor with the rest of his body.

45

THE SHOWDOWN

THE OPERATOR walks to the back corner of the empty casino and sits in Bacas's empty chair, his body exhausted. His eyelids snap shut for relief from the lights above. How many lights are there on the way to the pool hall? There is the one floodlight where the dogs fought—his eyes should be able to handle its brightness if he walks on the opposite side of the street. Are there others? He curses himself for not paying attention before the pain. The haze darkens the surface, but will it be enough for his eyes to last until he kills Bacas?

The scratch of claws against the floor comes from the front door and one eye shoots open. A rat scuffles into the room with a message on its back. If the rat is fed every time it delivers a message it must deliver a lot of messages. Every few steps the rat stops to sniff the air as it walks towards the back of the casino. When the rat reaches the Operator it scratches his foot, indicating the message is for him.

The Operator reaches down, grabs the message, and opens it. COME TO THE INTERSECTION OR YOUR FRIEND DIES.

The message is tossed on the table. The Operator lays his head on the back of the chair and closes his eyes as he takes long, steady breaths. Both fists clench at the thought of Miguel and the kinds of pain Bacas has inflicted on the old man. His jaw clenches when he remembers how Bacas sat in this very chair and killed Fenix as if the dog was just another wild rat. His thoughts turn to Patrice and how Bacas threatened to tell her secret to the world. Bacas deserves what he has coming to him.

The bloodstain on the floor is the first thing the Operator sees when he opens his eyes. Fenix barks somewhere in the back of his mind. It's time. How will he be able to kill the chief Enforcer without getting himself killed? Part of him wants to run through the door, run to the intersection with his gun drawn, and shoot without regard for his own life. The possibility of death before he eliminates Bacas is the only thing that stops him from being so cavalier. He isn't afraid to die, but he needs to make sure Bacas dies first.

Fenix's barks urge the Operator into action. The dull ache returns from the bright lights but, with his purpose clear, the pain doesn't register. The dead have themselves for company as they are left on the casino floor. Outside Suerte, instead of walking along the main street to the intersection, the Operator turns down a side street on his left. Two more right turns and he is able to see the intersection from the side opposite the station.

Bacas is in the intersection, a hooded Miguel as his human shield. They stand with their backs to the broken bridge on the left side of the intersection, the farthest from Suerte. The Operator darts across the street that runs parallel to the rails and waits to see if Bacas has any reinforcements who might have spotted him.

Nothing happens. Bacas still stands with Miguel between him and Suerte.

The Operator closes his eyes one final time before he crouches down and heads towards the intersection. He stays close to the building. The first rays of sunlight reach the ground and the pain in his eyes worsens. Time is running out. The Operator, now that he is closer, stands at full height and takes aim at the side of Bacas's head. The pain behind the Operator's eyes is almost unbearable.

From his right he sees the flash of a blaster from behind the skeleton of a car. "Watch out!" Manolo yells to Bacas.

The Operator turns his blaster and fires three quick shots into Manolo's chest. The man stumbles back and falls against the building behind him. Red streaks are left on the wall as he slides down. He had set up between the car and the building, ready to surprise the Operator from the left when his target walked from Suerte to the intersection.

Once the three shots have been fired, the Operator throws his arm up, blaster in hand, to shield his eyes from the light. Bacas turns to his right and repositions Miguel to keep his shield in front of him. Bacas points his own blaster at the Operator, confused.

"You killed all my men and now you stand there, exposed. Why?" Bacas says.

"Let him go," the Operator says in defiance. His arm still shields his eyes from the pain caused by the natural light.

"Him?" Bacas says with a laugh. "Who do you think this is?"

The Operator pulls his hand down and holds his blaster at his side. The light stabs his skull through squinted eyes. His words drip out, lacking the certainty he held a moment before. "Greyson told me you were at the pool hall."

"I was. His usefulness ran out. No, this is somebody else you wouldn't dare kill." The hood is ripped off the hostage and the Operator sees Patrice for what seems to him like the first time. A strip of white cloth gags her mouth and pins her dark brown hair to the back of her neck.

Rage wells up from deep within the Operator's stomach and

Fenix barks in his ear. He raises the blaster even though he can't see through the pain. All of a sudden there is an explosion in his knee and the pain in his eyes has found a companion.

"Once they found out she was an android they banished her from the upper levels. She was with her creator, who she still calls dad, when I told her you were with me. Naturally, she came at once."

"You shouldn't have come," the Operator says to Patrice through gritted teeth. His eyes are closed again as he tries to stand up. Without a kneecap for stability his leg gives out and he falls to the ground. His attempts to stand up are pointless; three times he tries and three times he falls. Bacas laughs louder with each failed attempt.

"Stay down," Bacas says.

The Operator gives up his struggle and lies down on the asphalt. Two pairs of footsteps shuffle on their way to him. With a big breath to gather himself he prepares for one final push. He props himself up on his left elbow, raises the blaster with his right arm, and opens his eyes to search through the cloud of pain for Bacas's head. Bacas fires first and the Operator feels his right elbow shatter. The blaster falls to the ground, useless, and so does he. His right arm hangs on by a thin thread of flesh.

"You just don't learn," Bacas sneers.

"Patrice!" a voice calls out from behind the Operator. "Don't hurt her!"

"Who are you?" Bacas says to the person behind the Operator.

"Her husband. Why are you doing this? Let her go!" the man says.

"There's a lot you don't understand," Bacas says to the husband.

"I'm not leaving without her," the husband says.

"This doesn't concern you," Bacas says. He turns back to the Operator on the ground.

"Patrice," the husband says, a plea to his wife. "I don't care if you're an android. I love you. We can live on the lower levels or even on the surface if we have to!"

Bacas walks closer to the Operator, with Patrice still between them. As he walks he shoots the Operator's other knee. The Operator grits his teeth, unwilling to give Bacas the satisfaction of hearing him scream.

"When this is all over," the Operator manages to open his eyes and say to Patrice, "I want you to forget about me. Leave with your husband and enjoy your life." The pain in his eyes pales in comparison to the pain in his joints, but he still has to close them soon after they open.

Bacas throws Patrice to the ground and fires two more shots, one in each of the Operator's ankles. This time the scream can't be held back.

Patrice's husband rushes to her side. "Pitiful. Even after she threw you away," Bacas says. His words are full of disdain, as if the sentiment is poison he must remove from his body. "Love is such a frivolous emotion. It causes you to do things even when it risks your own life. You two are a lot alike, you know. You rush to her side, she rushed to his."

The Operator wishes he could see her one last time but his eyes won't obey when he tells them to open. He remembers the blaster next to his left hand. "Bacas," he whispers.

Bacas takes a step forward. "Last request?"

The Operator is pretty sure he could hit him with a shot but he needs to be positive. There won't be a second chance.

"Bacas," he whispers again.

Bacas stands in front of the Operator's feet, his shadow cast in front of the Operator's eyes. Fenix growls.

"Any last words?" Bacas says.

"No!" Patrice screams. Her husband must have removed the gag from her mouth. "Let me go," she screams, as the man who loves her tries to hold her back from attacking Bacas.

Bacas laughs. Fenix barks. The Operator knows it's time. He lunges for the blaster with his last good limb and points it to the source of the shadow. He opens his eyes at the last possible second and pulls the trigger.

46

THE DECLARATION

"I won't lose you again," Patrice says through sobs. Her words, muffled and distant, reach the Operator through the pain that fills his head. Her voice doesn't have the same sweet melody he remembers. Hands on his shoulders lift him off the ground, and his head bounces from side to side with every shake of his exhausted body. "Wake up!" a frantic Patrice says.

Bile reaches the back of the Operator's throat. Between the shaking and the pain in his arms and legs he could vomit at any moment. "Leave," he whispers to Patrice, "before the government gets here."

"The government? What do they have to do with this?" she says.

The husband speaks up from where he stands behind Patrice. "The government will want to know how these men ended up dead. He will be taken into custody. There's nothing you can do for him."

Patrice leans over and wraps her arms around the Operator. She leans close, her mouth next to his ear. "I want to stay with you," she says.

The husband walks away to give them space.

"No you don't," the Operator says. "The government could take you into custody too. They would wipe your memory and reprogram you to work for them. You would have sacrificed your future and your past for nothing."

"For you! I would have sacrificed for you," Patrice whispers. Tears fall from her eyes and drip from her chin onto the Operator's face.

"Nothing good can come if you stay. You know now, right? You're an android. Do you really think we could be together? No." The Operator turns his head away and Patrice lets go of his shoulders.

"I lost you once. I'm not losing you again," she says, defiant.

The Operator wishes he could open his eyes and look at her face. His head stays turned away from the temptation. "We both know you belong with him. You have a happy life together. A life I thought I wanted with you, once upon a time. If you stay with me you'll grow to hate me. This isn't the life you want."

"But I would have you! Having you is enough for me," Patrice says. She has given up trying to keep her voice down in order to spare her husband's feelings.

"We will both have our memories of the time we spent together. Nobody can take that away from us. But soon, if you don't leave, you will lose both me *and* your freedom. I will be fine with whatever they do to me, but if I knew you had to suffer because of me I don't think I could handle it. Do this one last thing. For me."

More tears fall onto the side of the Operator's face. "Why did you leave? I was so alone."

"I had to, Patrice, I didn't know how else to handle it. I hated you for a long time but now I understand. This is the way it had to be. The way it *has* to be." The Operator turns his head towards the husband standing in the distance. He tries to open his eyes to get a look at her companion but the second his eyes experience their first ray of sunlight the pain almost causes him to pass out. "Get her out of here!" he yells to the man. "And hurry. The government will be here any second now."

Patrice leans over and gives the Operator a kiss, the final touch between two people who once meant so much to each other. The taste of salt lingers long after they part.

The husband pulls Patrice to her feet. The Operator tucks his chin and opens his eyes to get one final look at her as she walks away. Their shadows are all he sees before the pain behind his eyes causes him to pass out.

The Operator is pulled across the pavement by his left arm. There is no will left to fight. He faced his addiction and was able to resist, the final test to whether or not he was in control. Anything they do to him now doesn't matter. He resigns himself to whatever fate has in store for him. He will face it the same way he has faced every other challenge thrown at him: grit his teeth and bear it.

A door creaks open and the Operator is thrown inside. His eyes are closed and his body limp as he is propped against a wall in a seated position. Artificial light smacks his face and he hears a familiar voice.

"Wake up, señor," Miguel says. The Operator opens his eyes just enough to see the bruised and battered face of the pool hall owner. "I have you now. You killed that scoundrel, just like you said you would!"

The Operator manages a smile. "He almost gave me a six-pack."

"I see that," Miguel says. "Don't worry, amigo, limbs are easy to replace. We have all the parts we need leftover from the two androids who came over from Sigma."

COULD YOU DO ME A FAVOR?

Please help other readers learn more about this book by leaving a rating and review!

Then head over to my website authormarcoshernandez.com and subscribe to my email list. You'll hear about upcoming releases and deals you don't want to miss!

Android City Chronicles

The Return of the Operator

Before Anyone Finds Out

Good Enough in a Pinch

———

The Edited Genome Trilogy

Awakening

Alternative

Absolution

———

Hispanic American Heritage Stories

The Education of a Wetback

Where They Burn Books

They Also Burn People

Demons in the Golden Empire

———

Indigenous Magic

Jesus Chan and the Return of Mayan Magic

ABOUT THE AUTHOR

Marcos Antonio Hernandez writes from the suburbs of Washington, D.C. An avid reader of both fiction and non-fiction, his favorite authors are Haruki Murakami and Philip K. Dick — in that order.

Marcos graduated from the University of Maryland, College Park with a degree in chemical engineering and a minor in physics. Since graduating, he has worked as a barista, a food scientist, and a CrossFit coach.

The Return of the Operator is Marcos's second novel.

authormarcoshernandez.com